Tamsin

Annie Seaton

Pentecost Island 4

DEDICATION

To the wonderful girlfriends

I have made through my writing... author and

readers alike!

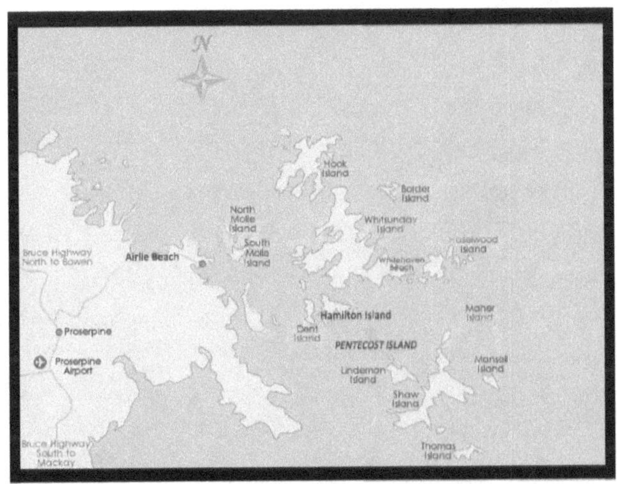

WHITSUNDAY ISLANDS

Chapter One

Tamsin

Tamsin Jones sprinkled corn starch over the surface of the large timber table and sent up a silent thank you to Pippa's Aunty Vi. It was a shame this table would go when the resort renovations were eventually done; it was the one thing she'd miss when she had a commercial kitchen with stainless steel benches. But it would be a while before she'd have to worry about that. The first few huts and the outdoor bar were about to open, and she would only be doing breakfasts on the veranda, and finger food in the bar from this old fashioned—but huge—kitchen in the 1930s house. Dinner would be delivered to the huts but cooking for six people at most each night would be easy.

Tipping the mixture onto the floured surface, Tam rolled the first ball of dough and kneaded it gently before dividing it into five equal portions.

Making pastry was soothing and she was enjoying working by herself. Things would change soon if she found it necessary to hire a kitchen hand to help prepare and clean up for the breakfast and bar trade. That depended on how the bookings went. It was an unknown, and she could tell that Pippa was beginning to stress. The informal bar launch had been a success, but that had been because of the yachties who were spending the winter in the islands. The girls had all been busy preparing for the official opening, and tempers had been short.

But Tam knew losing her solitude would be outweighed by having someone to clean up the kitchen. The work she'd been putting into the preparation for the opening next weekend had taken up most of her days and evenings, with little time for anything else. Having staff would leave her time for the creative work she loved. As she rolled the last of her pastry, Tam looked at her hands; they were dry from constantly being in dishwater for the past two weeks.

Pippa's voice drifted in from the veranda as she worked; Eliza's friend, Sienna, had taken her coffee out there a while ago.

Good, she wanted to see Pippa. There were a

few things Tam wanted to check about the opening. And apart from a brief hello to Sienna when she'd come in for coffee, Tam hadn't spoken to anyone else since last night. Nat and Nell had been closeted in the office and hadn't even come out for their coffee at ten as they usually did.

Tam hadn't minded the isolation since they'd arrived on the island six months ago. The first few months on the island with Pippa and Nell had been fun as they'd worked hard getting the house into a liveable condition. Then Eliza had arrived, soon followed by Evie. The two new arrivals had fitted into the dynamic, but—Tam bit her lip as she rolled out the second lot of pastry— since Eliza and Philippe had come back from Europe two days ago, there seemed to be even more tension in the air.

Maybe it was her imagination, she thought, carefully lifting the first circle of pastry and sprinkling it with corn starch. With a steady hand she gently placed each layer on top of the other until she had used the five circles.

With a satisfied nod, Tam rolled out the stack until it was about twice the diameter. The chicken and chilli filling was cooling in a saucepan on the stove and this was the last of the finger food to go into the big freezer.

Even though it was only midmorning, she yawned. She'd put in a hell of a lot of work and late nights to be ready for the opening. Being tired was the excuse she'd used for withdrawing a little over the past two days; the other girls had seemed to accept her distancing was due to being busy. Tam had almost filled the freezer that had been delivered from the mainland last month with finger foods and tapas. She was ready for the Turtle Bar opening in four days.

Even naming the bar had caused angst. Pippa had asked for suggestions, and then turned her nose up at each one. Three nights ago, Tam had lost it. 'You asked, we suggested. It's your bar, you name it!'

I need some time out, she thought. Without having to worry about Pippa's temper—and she had always had one—Tam was over trying to create exotic fillings; she was over being in the kitchen. This last lot of filled filo pastry cases would do it.

The pastry was perfect; she lifted it up and

stretched it slightly and then put it down on the table ready to cut the small circles to fill.

'Tam? Are you in there?' Pippa called from the veranda.

'Where else would I be?' Tam yelled back knowing her tone was snarky. As she turned to the door her elbow caught the bottle of olive oil that she'd used in the pastry.

'Damn.' Her mouth opened in horror as the bottle tipped and the oil spilled and spread into a large circle on the table.

All over the seven sheets of filo pastry she'd spent the last two hours perfecting.

'Bloody hell,' Tam screeched as she grabbed for the roll of paper towel and tried to mop up the oil. But it was too late; the pastry was ruined.

'What's wrong. What have you done?' Pippa's eyes widened as she looked at the glutinous mess on the table. 'Is that all? Thank goodness. I thought you'd cut or burned yourself.'

'Is that all?' Tam folded her arms and gritted her teeth as she stared at Pippa. '*That* is two hours of wasted work.'

'Oh well, you'll just have to start again,' Pippa said with a dismissive wave. 'Unless you can salvage *that*?'

Tam turned to look at Pippa— her friend, her boss and the owner of the island. Her voice was glacial. 'What did you say?'

'I said you'll have to do it again or I suppose you could do without it. Haven't you got enough food in the deep freeze already? You've been in this kitchen for days. We've hardly seen you since Eliza came home.'

Tam put her hands on her hips. 'Do you want to have food at the bar opening or not?'

'Okay, there's no need to get shitty,' Pippa replied. 'I just came down here to see if you had some bread in the freezer that I can take to Rafe's for lunch. We've run out.'

'I suppose Eliza and Philippe are up there for lunch too.'

Pippa's eyes narrowed. 'Yes, we're talking business. You're welcome to come up and have lunch with us. You know you're welcome at Rafe's any time. You've hardly been there since I moved out.

What's your problem?'

'Why do I have to have a problem?' This time it was Tam's turn to wave a dismissive hand. 'I have no right to have a problem with anything you do with *your* resort, Phillipa.'

'Jesus, Tam. What's crawled up your—'

'Just forget it.' Tam whipped off the apron that covered her shorts and T-shirt as she came to a quick decision. 'I didn't mean anything. I've got to go over to Hamo and get some disposable plates and serviettes for the opening. I'm going to have a bit of a break while I'm there.'

'That sounds like a good idea.' Pippa's voice was wary, but placatory. 'Why don't you come and have lunch with us? It sounds like you need a bit of company.'

'No. I've got to clean this mess up first.'

'Come up after you do that.'

'No, I'm fine. I'll get you some bread and you can go and entertain.' Tam knew she was being unreasonable but ruining the pastry had been the final straw.

It was the changes that were upsetting her.

Being tired didn't help and it had been ages since she and Pippa and Nell had watched the sunset with a bottle of bubbles. The fun had gone out of living here and now it seemed to be all work and no play.

It's a job, her subconscious told her. It's not supposed to be fun all the time. If Tam was honest, there *was* a bit of jealousy in the mix. Even though she was happy that Pippa and Rafe had announced their engagement, since Pip had moved up to Rafe's, the old house was not the same without her.

Pippa had been the one to hesitate, but it had been obvious Rafe wasn't going to give up.

Tam and Nell had both known it was only a matter of time before Pippa realised she was in love with Rafe, the author who owned half of the island. Her track record with men had not been good, but Pippa had finally accepted that she had found the right man this time.

A good man, Tam thought, and a patient one. Jeez, he'd have to be to put up with Pippa, she thought uncharitably.

The changes had left Tam feeling unsettled and now that Nat and Nell were mooning around each other, she hardly saw them either. That brought a smile to Tam's face; they were catching up on lost time because if they weren't in the office working on the network, the cabling, or going for a walk, they disappeared into Nell's bedroom early most evenings. Nat had his own room in one of the buildings behind the shed, but Tam suspected he didn't spend much time there. She didn't know if he was going to live on the island after the opening; or if he was helping in the bar on opening night. It hadn't been discussed—like a lot of things lately, it seemed. Gigi, the last person they had been going to hire had been a disaster and had only stayed on the island for a day.

If the truth be known Tam was lonely.

She looked up to see Pip looking at her with a curious look on her face. 'You okay, Tam?'

'Sorry I was shitty with you. I'm tired.'

'Do you want me to take you over to Hamo this afternoon?' Pippa reached out and put her hand on Tam's arm. 'Just chill, babe. It's all good. You've done a great job and I hope you know I've seen how much work you've put in, in the last few weeks. And how much I appreciate it.'

Tam settled a bit. 'Thanks, that'd be good if you can take me over today. Once I get this mess cleaned up and wash up, I'll have a shower and throw a change of clothes in a bag. The food's organised for the bar opening, but what do you think about me trying to find some temp staff while I'm over there? I know a couple of casual bar staff on Hamo who might be able to help on the night of the opening. We're also going to need someone to do the dishes, clear tables and clean up.'

'Yeah, Eliza and I were talking about that yesterday.'

'What did you decide? You and Eliza?' Tam scrubbed at the table with the paper towel.

Pippa folded her arms and leaned back on the table. 'That's one of the reasons I came down. I was going to make a time to talk to you about it.'

'So, talk to me.'

'Not while you're in a mood. I'll leave you to your cleaning up. The others are waiting for me. Just let me know when you're ready to go over to Hamo.'

'I'll text you and meet you at the boat.'

'Are you going to stay overnight?'

'Two nights,' Tam said making up her mind on the spot.

'Really? It seems silly to go away right before our big night. Are you sure you don't want to leave it until after Friday?'

'I'm sure.'

Pippa raised her eyebrows.

'Don't look at me like that, Pippa.' Tam put the cloth down. 'It's all right for you. This is your home, but it's my workplace. We've all worked hard for you, and I'm burning out. I just need some time to myself. Don't worry I'll be back Thursday, in plenty of time to get ready for Friday night.'

'Maybe I expect too much of you.'

'No, don't worry, it's just me.'

And a little bit of you too, Pippa, Tam thought. She couldn't pinpoint what had changed in the two days since Eliza and Philippe had come back to the island, but there was something. She had always been intuitive and there was something going on. As busy as Tam had been, Eliza had avoided her since their return. They were staying on Phillipe's boat and when she was on the island, Eliza hadn't even come down to say hello. They were always up at Rafe's.

Maybe she was being silly, but she couldn't help that niggle of jealousy at the thought that Eliza seemed to be muscling in on their friendship.

Don't be ridiculous, you're almost thirty-years-old, she told herself. It's not a playground friendship anymore; we're adults now, but even Pippa and Nell had had a huge blue last month, when Tam had acted as peacemaker.

'Okay, that's all good then,' Pippa said but her voice was clipped. Tam watched in disbelief as Pippa went over to the freezer, took out a loaf of bread and walked out the door without another word.

She threw the sodden paper towel in the bin, filled a jug with hot soapy water and chucked it on the table, not caring that it ran over the edge and onto the faded lino floor. Once the pastry had softened, she used a sharp spatula to scrape it off the wood surface and put it in the bin.

Her mood worsened and she muttered under her breath as she washed up. 'If we run out of food at the opening, that's just too friggin' bad.' She slammed the drawer shut as she put away the last of the cutlery. 'Maybe *Eliza* can come up with something.'

With one last look at the now spotless kitchen, Tam picked up the wet tea towels and headed out to the laundry at the end of the veranda. She threw them into the stone laundry tub and then sat down on the steps overlooking the back lawn and down to the garden that joined the rainforest. She drew in a deep breath and her temper slowly eased.

Evie had mowed that morning and the sweet smell of fresh cut grass took Tam back to her childhood in Brisbane. That smell always evoked a sense of nostalgia in her. She missed her family, and hardly saw them these days. Even before she'd moved north with Pippa and Nell, Tam hadn't seen them for over twelve months. Mum had headed off to Perth for a new job and Dad was somewhere up in the Northern Territory working on a cattle property. Her parents had been separated for many years but were still good mates and Tam kept in touch with both by email. But the smell of the grass took her back to those happy days of her childhood when they'd all lived together underneath Dad's parents' house in Brisbane. Times had been happy then, before her parents' love for each other had died. Her grandparents had passed away and the house with all the memories had been sold, and Tam had been a gypsy since then.

If there was one thing they'd taught her it was independence and Tam had achieved that in her late teens.

Living on the island and being part of Pippa's venture was a fabulous opportunity and a great way to live. She took another deep breath and leaned back on the veranda post.

What she had to understand was, it was Pippa's business and she was there to support her and look after the catering. Being in a snit and taking it out on Pippa and being jealous of Eliza was unnecessary and childish.

A couple of days away was just what the doctor ordered, and if she didn't get a move on, it would be too late to go today.

As Tam went to move, Evie came around the corner pushing the old hand push lawn mower that she'd discovered in Aunty Vi's shed.

'What's wrong with the ride-on?' Tam asked.

'Nothing, I like using this old one. It does a good job on the small patches of lawn. And it's quiet.' Evie pushed the mower to the door of the garden shed and came back over to Tam. 'What happened to you?'

Tam looked down and for the first time she noticed the big splotches of oil on her shirt. 'Nothing. Just an accident with a bottle of oil.'

Evie sat on the bottom step and yawned. 'It's been a big week. I've had it.'

'You and me both.' Tam smiled as an idea came to her. 'Hey, do you have anything planned for the next two days?'

'Only more mowing, But I'll probably leave that until Thursday and Friday morning, so it looks good on the day. The weather's looking good for the rest of the week. So no, nothing urgent. Why? Do you need a hand with something?'

'How would you feel about a couple of nights away? We've all been working hard.' Tam was tempted to add, 'some of us have, anyway' but she thought better of it.

'Tell me about it, Tam. I'm stuffed,' Evie said.

'You've worked so hard the place looks amazing. The lawns do too. Green and lush.'

'Yeah, it's coming together well. What did you mean about a couple of nights away? Where to?'

Tam stretched her legs out. The late morning sun was warm on her bare skin. She closed her eyes and thought about lying around a pool, a waiter bringing her a cocktail. Or two.

'I was just talking to Pippa. I'm going over to Hamo for a couple of days. I need to get some last minute supplies for Friday night, and chase up some casual kitchen staff but I've decided to take a couple of days break while I'm there. Why don't you come with me?'

Evie sat back and nodded slowly. 'That's the best idea I've heard for a long time. I'll take us over on my boat. Where were you going to stay? You could stay in the spare cabin on *Kestrel*.'

'Thanks for the offer but I'm craving a luxurious hotel room, with a spa bath and room service,' Tam said with a grin. 'I'm planning on getting dressed up—makeup, hair, nails the works. A dinner out at a restaurant, a few drinks and maybe a dance.'

'I can't afford the hotel room, but I'm happy to take you over and bunk down on my boat.' Evie touched her shoulder-length dark hair. 'And a haircut wouldn't go astray.'

'You can share a room with me if you want. I can get a twin.'

'No, if I'm paying for a marina berth, I'll stay on *Kestrel*. I miss being on the water.'

'Sounds good to me. Are you right to go soon?' Tam stood. 'I'll ring and book my room.'

'I can be ready in ten.' Evie jumped up. 'I'll bring her around to the wharf in an hour. That suit you?'

'Sure does.' Tam headed for her room.

After a quick hot shower, she spent more time on her hair than her usual pull-back-and-let it-dry style.

Tam took out her small suitcase and packed a few of her vintage dresses, her costume jewellery and her makeup. By the time she was ready to meet Evie, her mood had improved out of sight and her tiredness had been replaced with anticipation.

Chapter Two

Gabe

Gabe Kent walked out of the airport terminal on Hamilton Island and looked around. This was his first visit to North Queensland and so far, he liked what he saw—blue skies and sapphire waterways dotted with white sails. A warm breeze caressed his skin and happy chatter surrounded him as the crowd waited for the free electric buggies to take them to their accommodation.

He'd left Melbourne on a cold and windy September morning and stepped out of the jet to a spectacular sunny day. He reached up and loosened his tie, feeling decidedly overdressed.

Gabe had booked an apartment on Hamilton Island because he wasn't sure how long this job would take. If he had to travel around, a hotel was too expensive to use as a base—although his client was paying top dollar for this job so he could have booked a luxury apartment. He had more research to do and then had to wait until he could stay on Pentecost Island.

He'd called Ma Carmichael's, the new resort on Pentecost Island from Melbourne, and had tried to book accommodation there from this weekend, but the resort was about to open and was booked out for the first ten nights. He'd managed to get in after that for three nights. That would put him in close proximity to Tamsin Jones.

'They are self-contained huts, Mr Brown. Very simple, but with a bathroom, bedroom and small living area. Each hut overlooks the bay and has magnificent views. Breakfast will be served on the main veranda of the house and light meals will be served in the bar. If you place an order before noon each day, dinner can be delivered to your hut. The menus will be in the compendium.' The efficient receptionist had introduced herself as Nell. 'As you say your dates are flexible, I will add you to the wait list in case we have a cancellation and an earlier vacancy.'

'Thank you, Nell. I've heard you have an excellent chef on staff.'

There was a moment's hesitation before she answered. 'Yes, our chef, Tamsin, was highly regarded at Peppers at the Gold Coast when she was there.'

Bingo! Tamsin. It had to be her; it was an unusual name. He *was* on the right track.

'Excellent. Will there be food available at the bar opening this week?'

'Yes, I've seen the bar menu already. Tamsin has outdone herself for the opening. Would you like to make a booking? We're almost full.'

'Certainly. Is there a shuttle service to your island from Hamilton Island?'

Gabe had known there was the function on Friday night, and he was determined to be there even if he had to hire a boat.

'Yes. That's correct. Are you staying on Hamilton Island or the mainland?'

'Hamilton.'

'Good.' Nell gave him the number of the shuttle service.

'Thank you, Nell.'

'Thank you, Mr Brown. We'll look forward to seeing you on Friday night. Oh, and in case you didn't know, it's tropical or fancy dress for the opening.'

'Tropical?'

'Hawaiian shirt, boardshorts, that sort of thing. We're very informal here and it's a special night.'

'Sounds good to me. Thanks.'

'May I have your mobile to add to your reservation?'

Gabe reeled off the number of his second mobile. The one he used for work.

He was satisfied; the first opportunity to observe his target had been organised. Being in a crowd, it would make it much easier than some of the one on one observations he'd done on other cases.

The apartment he'd booked was a couple of streets up the hill from the shopping and restaurant precinct; he could walk down and eat at a restaurant each night and not have to worry about meals. If there was one thing Gabe hated, and didn't do well, it was cooking. His limit was a piece of toast, or opening a box of cereal, so if he could find a supermarket, he had breakfast covered.

The apartment had advertised fast and reliable

internet speed—and that was his priority. As long as he had that, a bed and a bathroom, and restaurants within walking distance, all bases were covered.

Gabe walked along the drive from the airport to the shopping precinct and absorbed the atmosphere. The connecting flight he'd boarded in Brisbane had been filled with happy holidaymakers in brightly-coloured clothes and he decided to ditch the suit as soon as he could.

Plus, he'd have to buy a Hawaiian shirt somewhere; he wasn't going to draw attention to himself in fancy dress. Sweat trickled down his neck; how could it be so much warmer up here? It was barely a month into spring. But he could deal with the heat; the air was pure and fresh, and the water looked inviting.

Shame he had to work. But he'd promised his client he would deliver, and Gabe had a one hundred percent track record in client satisfaction.

This case was cut and dried; it was only a matter of getting Tamsin Jones to tell the truth and cough up the goods.

Once he was sure she was the guilty party.

That was the first thing he had to establish.

***

An hour later Gabe had settled into his apartment. He'd come straight up the hill, ditched the suit and shoes and socks, changed into a pair of shorts and a T-shirt and headed down the hill to the grocery store. He'd been tempted to have a look around, but there wasn't time yet, so he'd stocked up on coffee, milk and cereal, a few snacks and a six-pack of beer.

He went straight back to the apartment and put away the groceries before pulling out his laptop and setting up on the balcony facing the water.

Maybe not such a good idea. The view was enticing, and he sat there for a few minutes watching a guy on a sailboard. Looked like fun. He'd have a go at that before he left. Gabe knew he'd spent way too much time working over the past five years, and he hadn't taken a break. He was almost in a good enough financial position to give the job away, and if he cracked this case, he'd be looking at moving north and buying some property. If he cracked this case, his life would change.

Sitting in the sun watching the water isn't

going to achieve much, he told himself; there was no time for relaxation yet. He had work to do.

But maybe after he'd completed his task, and his client was happy and the item in question had been returned to its rightful owner, maybe he'd have a week or so up here and look around. The prospect of returning to Melbourne didn't appeal at all.

Gabe connected to the apartment's network and logged into his email account. There was an email from Lukas Werner with some more details about Tamsin Jones; her employment dates and a couple of references that Lukas had found in the business files, but they wouldn't help him much.

With a frown, Gabe switched to code and began a background and asset check on his quarry.

Chapter Three

Tamsin

After she'd packed, Tam had gone out to the veranda to call Pippa. It seemed strange to have to ring or text each other now, when they'd lived in close quarters since they'd arrived on the island.

Pippa didn't come down to the old house as often now and Tam knew the tight strands of their friendship were unravelling. Every few days Pippa would run in and stick her head in the door and call out, 'everything okay?' but she never stayed around to chat for long.

It was as though their relationship had moved to a more formal employer-employee one, even though the change hadn't been discussed.

She liked Nell's idea of the three of them getting together for drinks on Thursday night; they needed to touch base and get back to that easy friendship they'd had for so long.

Okay, so Nell and Pippa had partners now; it didn't mean their friendship had to change; it was too precious to let go. It wasn't the arrival of Rafe and

Nat that had changed the way things were; Tam knew it was the imminent opening of the resort that was causing the tension.

Pippa picked up the call straight away. 'Hi Tam. You're right to go?'

'Yeah, but I don't need you now. Evie's taking me over. She's going to have a couple of days off too.'

'Oh.' Then silence.

'Come on, Pip. She's been working like a Trojan. Did you want us to put in a leave application or ask permission?' Tam burred up. 'I didn't think we worked like that, *boss.*' She frowned as the words spewed out. What was happening to her? When Pippa had been a cow to Nell about the secret she'd held to herself for ten years, Tam had been the one to keep calm. Now she felt as though *she* was in Pippa's firing line.

'I didn't mean that. I meant, "oh" as in I was disappointed because I was hoping you and I could have a chat on the way over. Never mind. And listen it's okay. Of course, I don't mind you taking time out. You know how we work. I trust you. I'm just surprised that you're going away so close to the opening.'

'I'm all organised, Pip. And I'll go stir crazy if I spend one more hour in that kitchen. We'll be back Thursday morning. Evie has to finish the lawns before Friday, and I'll take most of Friday to get the food down to the bar. Nat's going to get the drinks and glasses sorted.'

'Okay, have a good break. We'll catch up when you get back. Nell rang and told me about sunset drinks on Thursday.'

'Yeah, just the three of us. It'll be like when we first arrived.'

'I've already told Eliza about it. She was keen when I mentioned it.'

'Whatever,' Tam said, and she knew her voice was short.

'And it would be rude not to invite Evie and Sienna too,' Pippa added.

'You're the boss. Do what you want.'

'Tam? Do me a favour? Have a break and chill. You're strung out.'

She ignored Pippa's concern. Or was it

criticism? 'Is there anything you want from Hamo?'

'No. Nothing, I can think of, but I'll call you if I think of anything.'

'I'll see you Thursday afternoon.'

'Okay, take care. And, Tam? Make sure you have a good break.'

'I will.'

As she disconnected, Tam looked up as the hammock at the end of the veranda moved. Sienna was swinging in the canvas chair.

'Morning, Sienna, I didn't see you there.'

Sienna stood and stretched her arms above her head. Tam felt dowdy beside her, even though she had put on one of her favourite vintage dresses. Surprisingly it was a little bit looser; she'd been working so hard she must have lost some weight. Her hair was out, but her blonde curls were in a tangle. She desperately needed a cut and foils, and her nails and hands needed attention.

Ever since Sienna had arrived on the island with Eliza and Philippe, she'd always looked elegant and well-groomed.

Her glossy auburn hair fell in a perfect bob

that brushed her graceful neck. She wore long, loose silk pants, and sleeveless tops in jewel-like colours, and her makeup was always meticulously applied. Even at breakfast.

She reminded Tam of Mrs Werner at the jewellery store where she'd worked at Pacific Fair. That certain European style—elegance. No matter how hard Tam tried, she knew she'd never attain that level of elegance or sophistication. But Sienna seemed to achieve it effortlessly; she was always perfectly groomed and ladylike. Despite that, she had no airs and graces. Friendly and always willing to chat she had already offered to help Tam in the kitchen already.

Despite her pretty dress, Tam felt fat and frumpy beside Sienna; Pippa and Nell had always told her she was feminine and curvy, but Tam knew she was just plain plump. How could you not be overweight working with food all day?

'I don't know if it's jet lag or just this island atmosphere, but every time I sit in that chair, I seem to drift off to sleep,' Sienna said.

'Half your luck. I don't think I've even tried

one of them out yet.'

Eliza had suggested the hammocks before she went away, and Pippa had brought six of the cream hammock chairs back from the mainland a couple of weeks ago. Three for the veranda, and one each for the huts. Rafe had secured each to a hook in the ceilings. The tasselled ropes and colourful throw rugs, along with the black pots filled with bright flowers that Evie had placed along the edge of the verandas made the outside of the house look inviting. It would be different once the resort opened and strangers would be making themselves at home.

'I feel guilty lounging around while you're all working so hard,' Sienna said.

'Don't be silly. You're on a holiday.'

'I'd love to work on the island like you all do. You're so lucky to live here.'

Tam nodded. 'We are.'

'It's so beautiful, isn't it?' Sienna gestured out to the calm water. There was no wind today and the Whitsunday Passage glowed with silver in the late morning sun. 'I've spent a lot of time in the Mediterranean, but you know what? It's even prettier here than the Greek Islands.'

'Where are you from? I can't place your accent.'

'Switzerland. Lucerne. I grew up in a house on the lake, so I always feel at home when I'm near the water.'

'How did you meet Eliza?'

'We went to boarding school together in England.' Sienna stared out over the water. 'I still feel guilty that I didn't stop her marrying Rocco. We were together in Florence on a holiday when she met him.'

'People have to take responsibility for their own actions. You can't make decisions for them.' Tam pushed away the memories of Chad that suddenly surfaced.

Practise what you preach, she thought. That was in the past.

Another thought struck her as Sienna stood and picked up her coffee cup from the small table.

'Hey, do you want to come and see more of the islands? Evie and I are going over to Hamo for a couple of days.'

'Hamo?' Sienna tilted her head to the side and

her nose wrinkled as she frowned.

Tam chuckled. 'Hamilton Island. Sorry, local lingo. Did you hear me tell Pip we are taking a couple of days break? You're quite welcome to share a room with me, or if you want, we can book a single room for you.'

'I didn't hear, but I'd love to.'

'Evie's going to stay on her boat in the marina, so I'd appreciate the company.'

Sienna nodded and her smile was wide. 'Sounds good to me. I've been a bit lonely the last couple of days. Eliza's been up at Pippa's talking business non-stop.'

Tam pushed back that niggle of jealousy. It was *business*. There was no need to feel as though Eliza was pushing them out, but it was a bit rude to leave Sienna abandoned when the rest of them were so busy. They each had their roles, and if what Eliza was talking to Pippa about improved the business, that was good.

It was.

'How long until you leave?' Sienna asked.

'I'm packed. Evie's bringing the boat around

to the jetty in about ten minutes. How long will it take you to get ready? We can wait.'

'I can collect my bag and be ready in about three minutes,' Sienna said. 'I won't have time to go up to Rafe's, so I'll just give Eliza a call and let her know what I'm doing. I'd hate them to think I've gone missing.'

'I'll wait out here while you get packed.' Tam grinned. 'I'm pleased you're coming with us. This is turning into a party.'

When Sienna hurried back to her room, Tam sat in the hammock. It would be good to have some female company. Go out, have a few drinks, have a meal and let her hair down.

And have a manicure and visit the hairdresser. While she waited, she dialled the salon at Hamo, and was pleased to pick up a cancelled spot that afternoon.

There was a new restaurant on Hamo that was getting excellent reviews on their Facebook page; she was looking forward to trying Stonehaven and getting some ideas, but she wouldn't book until she checked that the others were happy to go there. It was an expensive place and she was conscious of what Evie had said about not being able to afford to stay in a room at the hotel.

Evie had stayed at the house occasionally over the past few weeks; her yacht was moored around in Back Bay, and it saved her coming over in the dinghy each morning, but she said it didn't feel right to sleep at night without the floor rocking.

'I feel guilty having you live on your boat while there's a perfectly good room in the house here for you,' Pippa had said.

Evie had shaken her head. 'I've lived on *Kestrel* for ten years now. I guess, as well as loving the feel of the water rocking me off to sleep, I do feel a little bit claustrophobic when I'm in a house. Four walls and all that. On my boat, there's space and freedom.'

Tam had been on Evie's boat a couple of times and she certainly wouldn't describe the tiny cabins, the toilet in a cupboard and the deck shower as space and freedom. She liked her creature comforts too much.

As she rocked in the hammock, Tam

wondered how long Evie would stay on Pentecost Island. She was a whiz at landscape design, and the gardens, house verandas and huts looked a picture. They didn't know a lot about Evie; she was never very forthcoming about what she'd done since they'd known her at uni. All they knew was she lived on her boat and worked her way around the islands. Somewhere along the line she had got her landscaping qualifications and enough experience to design a showpiece resort here. She'd certainly made a difference to the development of the island, and even though she didn't reveal much about herself, she was fun to work with.

We all have our secrets, Tam mused.

'I'm ready.' Sienna came out of the house carrying two large bags.

Tam chuckled. 'No offense, love, but we'll only be away two nights.'

Sienna smiled back. 'You'll see what I have packed when we get there. I have a treat for you and Evie.'

As they walked down to the wharf Tam looked around the island, trying to imagine what the island would look like to first-time visitors when they arrived. Since they'd moved here, she'd gotten used to the place.

Pentecost Island was ninety percent mountain. She'd never forget the first sight of the peak rearing up from the sea when Jiminy brought them over in his boat last autumn.

Along the eastern and western sides of the island was a flat shoreline edged by sand; the narrow grassy plain then climbed to small foothills beneath the mountain that comprised most of the island. Along the entire western end of the island where Aunty Vi's house, the huts and the bar were, Evie had already made a difference. Around the house, the lawn was lush and green, and she mowed every few days. Winding paths wound their way from the house into the rainforest. Evie had added hanging birdfeeders to the trees that edged the lawn, and the birdsong at sunrise was a pleasure to hear.

Additional to the one overgrown path that had been the only access to the beach when they'd first arrived, there were now four paths heading off to small glades where Evie had made fallen logs into seats and tables and created small gardens around the base of the trees.

Even though the cleared glades were small, along with the beach and the cleared pockets of rainforest there would be enough places for guests to find somewhere private to relax. As she and Sienna walked through one small glade on their way to the wharf, Tam spoke her thoughts aloud.

'I could do lunch picnic baskets for the guests.'

'You could. If you ever need a hand in your kitchen, please ask,' Sienna offered. 'I'd love to help.'

'I'll take you up on that, especially at the end of the week. It's going to be madness for the bar opening.'

'Just ask. I'll be pleased to help out.'

'How pretty,' Sienna exclaimed when they reached the huts. 'The gardens and pots weren't here when we arrived.'

Evie had cleared a patch of bush, and a tiny patch of lawn at the back of each hut joined the rainforest and a path led into the main glade. At the front, there was a small square pebbled area with a table and two chairs and pots with brightly coloured tropical flowers spilling out over onto the pebbles.

'Evie's done a great job,' Tam said. 'She's been a great addition to the island.'

Sienna paused and looked at the gardens. 'Does she do all of this herself?'

'Yes. Every time Pip offered to get someone to help her with the heavy labouring work Evie said she'd rather do it herself. Rafe and Phillipe have helped with some of the heavy lifting, but most of the time she does it.'

'I can understand that.' Sienna joined Tam as they stepped onto the beach. 'I prefer to work by myself and go at my own speed. If I had to think about what I had to tell somebody to do all day it would interrupt my workflow. I don't have to worry about anyone else in my salon. I always allocate two hours for my clients too, and they seem to enjoy it. I hate rushing.'

Maybe that was Sienna's secret to looking elegant. Tam thought of her work and grinned. No chance of relaxing when there were orders coming in and going out at a rate of knots. But she loved the pace of her work now that she was working with food again; she hadn't been too upset when the jewellery store she had worked on at the Gold Coast had closed. The Werners had been a wonderful couple to work for, but when it wasn't busy, it had been boring work. You could only polish glass showcases so many times before it became a mindless activity. The clientele there had not been her sort of people either. Who could really spend that much on what was essentially a lump of rock?

'You're a beauty therapist?' she asked Sienna.

'I am.' Sienna smiled and lifted one of the bags she was carrying. 'I'm going to give you and Evie a treat. That's if you want one.'

'Oh, yes please.' Tam held her hands up. 'I've booked the hairdresser. And I was going to book a manicure and a facial too.'

'I can do both for you.'

'Great. And I'll pay for our room. That's a fair deal.'

Sienna smiled and pointed to the wharf. 'That's Evie's boat?'

'It is.'

Evie was on the foredeck of *Kestrel*, and Tam almost did a double take. The usual khaki work pants and work shirt had been replaced by a pale blue dress that contrasted with Evie's tanned skin. She'd pulled her dark hair into a high ponytail and was wearing a chunky bead necklace around her neck, and dangling earrings to match.

'You look ready to party, Evie, and guess what? Sienna's coming with us, too,' Tam said.

'Excellent. The more the merrier,' Evie replied as she took their bags over the side and put them on the deck of the small boat.

'You do look very lovely, Evie,' Sienna said.

Evie chuckled. 'It's good to get out of the work clothes every so often. So, come aboard, gals, and we'll get going. I'm really looking forward to having a couple of days off.'

Sienna stepped on board the yacht. 'I've not spent much time on boats before.'

'Sit up the front. Are you in a hurry, Tam? I thought we'd sail over.'

'As long as I'm there in time to drop my bag

off at the hotel and get to a three o'clock hair appointment, I've got all the time in the world,' Tam said.

'It'll only take us an hour under sail. There's just enough wind to push us along and the tide's ebbing to the north so that'll give us some speed too.' Evie pulled a face and held up her hands. 'Hair appointment sounds good. I might even look for a manicure although I think my poor hands are beyond redemption.'

Tam smiled at Sienna. 'We're all set, Evie. We have our own personal manicurist and beauty therapist on board.' She was about to step onto the boat when she noticed Nell walking along the beach to the jetty.

'That sounds great,' Evie said with a smile and Tam thought how pretty she looked today.

'And then tonight when we're all glammed up, we'll hit the bar and restaurants if you're both happy to go out.'

'You bet.' Evie nodded. 'Let's go party, girls! Come on Tam, or we'll go without you.'

'I'm just waiting to see what Nell wants.'

'Have a great time, you three.' Nell said as she stepped onto the jetty. Nat was sitting on the rocks at the northern end of the beach. 'If I wasn't taking the accommodation bookings, I'd think about coming with you. Sounds like a great time's been planned.'

Tam chuckled. 'You could come. You could leave Nat to man the phones.'

Nell looked coy. 'Yeah, but I'd miss him.'

'You pair are hopeless.' Tam rolled her eyes, but she reached out and hugged Nell. 'Young love, nothing like it. I'm happy for you.'

'Not so young these days. You'd better hurry up and find yourself a fella, Tamsin.' There was sympathy in Nell's expression. She alone knew about Tam's experience at Peppers and why she'd left her job to go and work in a jewellery store for a couple of years before they'd moved up to Pentecost Island.

'You know me, Nell. I've no intention of ever settling with one man, and even if I wanted to, there's not much chance of that when I'm in a kitchen by myself all day long.'

'You love it. And besides there's going to be a

lot more people on the island soon. You never know who you'll meet. When you meet the right one, you'll soon change your mind. Look at me.'

Tam spoke quietly. 'You know that's never going to happen.' She tapped the side of her nose. 'But between you and me, Nellie, I'll be looking for a good time while I'm on Hamo.'

Nell blushed. 'Tamsin!'

'Love ya, Nellie girl! You never change. See you on Thursday.' Tam stepped off the jetty onto Evie's yacht. 'Come on girls, let's get this party underway.'

Chapter Four

Pippa

The ice tinkled in the pretty blue jug as Rafe poured our drinks. I'd made sandwiches for the four of us. Eliza's request to have a formal meeting had me intrigued.

When I'd come up the hill I'd been out of sorts, worrying about Tam. In all the years we'd been friends I'd never seen her act like that, and it worried me. I tried to put it behind me as I leaned back in my chair and sipped the lemon drink Rafe had poured.

'It's much nicer outside than in on a lovely day like this,' I said when Eliza and Philippe joined us. I had insisted they stay in one of the huts last night when Eliza had said they were happy to stay on the boat.

'No, it's fitting. You just about built those huts singlehandedly, and it's a good trial run for them before the guests arrive. You can check that we furnished them properly while you were away. Make sure we have all the little touches in them. None of us have really got interior design skills so I want an honest appraisal. Okay?'

'I can do that,' Eliza had agreed.

Phillipe held the chair out for Eliza to sit at the table and the wind lifted her dark hair.

'You'll be pleased to know we had a very pleasant night,' she said. 'The bed was comfortable, and there's nothing I could add to make the room better.'

'How was the water pressure?' Rafe asked. 'We had a bit of trouble with that.'

'Perfect,' Eliza said. 'And the compendium is great. You've done well, Pippa. Having dinners taken to the hut is a good idea until the restaurant gets going.'

'Yes, it will be a while before we can afford to build the proper commercial kitchen. We've brought the one in the house up to standard, but it's not big enough to cater for a restaurant.'

'When are the first guests in?'

'Saturday. The night after the bar opening,' I said. 'I know I've left the staffing way too late, but I've got a couple of women coming over tomorrow to interview for the housemaid positions. If they're not suitable, Rafe and I will be housemaids until we get someone.'

Phillippe chuckled. 'Rafe, you are a good man.'

'Will the housemaids stay on the island too?' Eliza asked.

I put my drink on the table as Rafe sat beside me and shook my head. 'No. I've organised with Jiminy to do a pickup at ten o'clock each morning to pick up the outgoing guests, and the staff will come over from Hamo with him, and then he'll come back at two with the incoming guests for that night and take them back. It's a bit of an organisational nightmare because we'll have to have the rooms cleaned after the guests leave, even if we haven't got anyone new coming in. Nell's got it in hand though. She's a great organiser.'

'How are the bookings?' Eliza asked.

'The three huts are already booked out for the first ten nights.'

'That's fantastic.' Eliza shot a glance at Philippe before she turned back to Rafe and I. 'Have you given much thought to building more huts yet?

Expanding further along the shore?'

'We've talked about it but nothing concrete yet.'

'We've got a proposition for you.' Eliza reached out and put her hand on Pippa's arm. 'I hope we're not overstepping the mark.'

I sat back ready to listen. Over the past couple of weeks, it was as though the resort had taken on a life of its own. I wasn't sure how I felt about that, or whether I was even ready. My dream of creating a small resort out of my inheritance had grown legs and seemed to be up and running by itself.

What had started out as an adventure with Nell and Tam was growing bigger than I'd ever imagined, and fast.

'You look worried, Pippa,' Eliza said.

'No, I was just thinking how quickly we've grown. Tell me what you're thinking.'

Rafe leaned forward and his voice held a note of warning. 'I'm here to support Pippa and I'm willing to support anything that *she* wants.'

'Thanks, love. Let's listen.'

And I was prepared to listen. I knew I had

some work to do. Tam was not happy, and I knew her being unsettled was more than her having to work in difficult conditions in the old kitchen. I knew she had a problem with Eliza since they'd returned, and I didn't know why. They'd got on fine when Eliza was here building the first three huts.

'Okay, fire away.

Eliza hesitated. 'You know my story and how I got here. And how I met Philippe.' He reached over and put his arm around her. She seemed nervous and that was out of character.

'We had a meeting with Rocco's lawyer in Florence, and the estate is tied up in a tangle of companies and restrictions, and criminal investigations. I don't want anything to do with it. Apparently, he was involved in quite a bit of underhanded stuff.'

Phillipe nodded. 'He was a liar and a cheat, and I was horrified when I met Eliza in Croatia. I quickly realised she didn't know what he was like. She wasn't even aware he'd been married before.'

'No. I found that out later. Along with many more things that were horrifying.' Eliza's voice shook a little. 'What we did find out in Florence—and what I'll use if you like my suggestions, is that as soon as we were married, he'd put the villa in Tuscany under my name, and put it on the market.

'Apparently, he knew he was under investigation, and he needed some quick cash. Having it in my name cleared it from any legal hold-ups or freezing of his assets.'

'So, you own a villa in Tuscany?' Rafe asked.

'No, it had already sold, and the money was in the account that he had set up in my name.'

I was happy for Eliza. 'I guess it's some compensation for what you went through and how you had to change your identity.'

'It's left me absolutely stunned, and I just wanted to get back here as quickly as I could to tell you about it. All of you, but everyone is busy here, and now Tam and Evie have taken off for a few days. And I've barely seen Nell since we arrived.' Eliza's dark eyes were wide as she stared at me.

'What did you mean by your suggestion?' I asked.

'I want to invest in your resort, Pippa. I want

to help you set it up like you dreamed it would be.'

'I'd have to think about that, I guess,' I said slowly.

'Do you have a business plan?' Philippe asked.

'Yes, of course I do. I know what I want to do here but most of it's a dream. It'll take years until we make enough to put that sort of money back in. At the moment we have to do up the kitchen and maybe add a couple of huts.'

Rafe leaned forward and put his arm around Pippa. 'Am I rude—and please tell me if I'm overstepping here—in asking how much you want to invest? I imagine that will have a lot to do with your decision, love?'

'It would. And also, the vision you have for the resort would have to be in line with mine,' I said.

'My plan is that I just put the money in as a silent partner and you follow your original dream—or business plan—' Eliza flicked a smile at Philippe, and he reached over and took her hand in his. 'We're going to be doing a lot of travelling in Phillipe's boat in a year or so.' She chuckled and put on her Cockney accent. 'If anyone had ever told me I'd end up with a sailor I would have said they were Patrick Swayze.'

I frowned and looked at Philippe. 'Patrick Swayze? You don't look a bit like him.'

He shrugged in a very French way. 'When she reverts to her language, I have trouble with understanding her too.'

'God, you lot.' Eliza rolled her eyes, and I was pleased to see her relax. She had been holding herself tense as she spoke. 'You know? Crazy? Patrick Swayze, Crazy. Rhyming slang. I'm a Cockney, m'dears.' Eliza's levity lightened the mood that had been building and I laughed.

'It's so good to have you back. Both of you,' I said. 'I mean that. So, tell me what Rafe asked. How much are you talking about? A few thousand to build some more prefab huts? Or a bit more that we could maybe upgrade our boat with?'

Eliza lifted her chin and took a deep breath and as she spoke, my jaw dropped.

'To be equal partners, we would match the value of the island, and the resort and the business. I would say that that would be well over a million dollars. We'd have to get it formally valued.'

'Bloody hell!' I stood up and looked down at Eliza. 'How much did the villa sell for?'

'Um, two million euros was in my account in Italy. We arranged the transfer to an Australian account when we landed in Brisbane.'

'That means nothing to me. What is that in dollars, please?'

Rafe tugged at my hand and I sat back down. 'That, my dear, is approximately three million dollars.'

I fanned myself with both my hands and my voice squeaked. 'And you want to put a million dollars into the resort?'

Eliza nodded and her smile was wide. 'I do. Very much so. I was so excited when we came back and I wanted to run in and tell you as soon as I stepped foot on Pentecost Island. I hope you agree. Please, sweetie. I owe you all so much. If it wasn't for Tam, I would have drowned that night. You let me hide out on the island until I found out Rocco was dead, and then you looked after me.' Her large dark eyes filled with tears.

'And not just you, Pippa. Nell and Tam were a big part of my recovery. I want to allocate a share of my money to each of them so they are also partners in the business.'

'I just don't know what to say.' I slumped back into my chair, absolutely overwhelmed.

'It's easy. Just say yes.' Eliza's fingers were white where she was gripping the arm of her chair.

'Are you sure you really want to do this?' I stood again and walked around to her side of the table. 'There's a lot more in the world to spend that sort of money on.'

'There might be, but Pentecost Island is where I want to settle, and this is where I want to call home.'

I grabbed Eliza's hands and pulled her up. 'Well, subject to the valuation and that you really are sure you mean this, the answer is . . . yes!'

She screeched and threw her arms around me. 'Oh my God, I can't believe it. I wasn't sure how you'd take it.'

I hugged her and we were almost dancing on the spot, as we jiggled and laughed and squealed. I turned to Rafe with the widest grin.

'Sweetheart, I think bubbles are in order.'

'I think so too.' He stood and came over and hugged both of us and headed inside followed closely by Philippe. 'You are a lovely soul, Eliza,' he said.

I put my forehead against Eliza's. 'You are the kindest friend. I simply cannot believe your generosity.' I felt her head shake slightly next to mine.

'No, it was the care that you all gave me when I needed it. That's what I'll never forget. This is not money that I earned or that I would ever have had, so I want to do something with it that pays you all back.'

'You don't have to, you know.'

'I know that, but I want to.'

I let go of her and stepped back. 'I can't wait until you tell Nell and Tam, but let's wait until the girls come back from Hamo. We'll tell them at sunset on Thursday.'

'Pippa? There's just one thing I'd like to ask you. It would mean a lot to me.'

I tipped my head to the side. 'Yes?'

'You talked about a day spa on the island. I'd

really love to see that go ahead as part of this, and if you're happy, offer the job to Sienna. She's a wonderful person, and really good in her field, and I know she'll fit in with the girls. She should be able to get a working visa to start with.'

I laughed. 'That sounds great, and she does get on with us all. She's already taken off with Tam and Evie.'

My earlier uncertainty had evaporated, and I was excited about the future of our island.

'The girls are going to be absolutely . . .'

'Gobsmacked!' Eliza's grin was as wide as mine.

Chapter Five

Tam stood on the back deck of Evie's yacht as they motored through the narrow channel between the coral heads and headed towards open water. Nat and Nell were walking along the beach hand-in-hand and they waved madly, and the girls waved back. Tam looked up to the hill on the south side of the bay; they were still close enough to see the two couples on the balcony at Rafe's house, but no one noticed them motoring out of the bay.

Or acknowledged us, anyway.

You're obsessing, she told herself. And if she was honest, she was jealous and a little bit frustrated. Pippa and Nell being in relationships had her feeling lonely; she probably owed Pippa an apology. Her crankiness had been a bit over the top, but mind you, Pippa always gave back as good as she got.

Tam smiled again at Nell's reaction to her "looking for a good time". Maybe she'd meet a good-looking tourist who was looking for a holiday fling.

That would suit her just fine, get rid of her frustration and restore her equilibrium. Hopefully she'd come back a lot more mellow.

Already feeling better as the island quickly receded into the distance, Tam moved her gaze away from Rafe's house. From her vantage point at the back of the yacht the island looked a picture. It was much easier to see Aunty Vi's old house now; Rafe had helped Pippa paint the outside. He was between books and had spare time for a month or so. Pippa was a lucky woman; Rafe was a top guy and he adored her.

Tam just hoped Pip didn't stuff up this relationship as she had with her others.

The front of the house where the main veranda wrapped around to the western side was now painted white and contrasted with the old-fashioned red roof. From this distance, the rust blended in and the roof glowed red in the midday sun. Evie had suspended baskets of brightly coloured flowers from the outside of the veranda posts. The flowers and the white house contrasted with the green lawns. The first view tourists would get of the island was enticing.

Evie had placed two huge urns on each side of the wide steps that led up to the front veranda and filled them with red and white flowers. Tam moved her gaze along the beach; the three huts that were hosting their first guests this weekend stood like sentinels on the shore, they too were surrounded with colourful flowers. She stood there alone and stared across the water as Pentecost Island receded into the distance. From here it simply looked like the volcano she had first seen; you wouldn't think there was a small resort on it now. They had created something to be very proud of, and Tam crossed her fingers that it was successful for Pippa.

She had fallen in love with the place; it would be very hard to leave if she ever decided to move on. *Maybe I'll still be here in my dotage like Pippa's Aunty Vi.*

'This island resort of yours is going to be an incredible success.' Sienna must have read her mind as she moved to stand beside her. 'I can already feel peace and serenity trickling into me.'

Tam laughed. 'I can feel peace and serenity trickling into me the further I get away from the island today. I'm pleased it's a good holiday for you, but it's been many hours of work for us. Don't get me wrong, I do love it. I just needed a break. But it is a wonderful place to live and the work is satisfying,' she added. 'Extremely satisfying and it will be even more so when we get real guests next week.'

Tam *was* serene when they approached the marina at Hamilton Island. Evie had put the mainsail up, and turned the motor off, and the boat had skimmed over the sea with barely a sound. The occasional slap of a wave on the side, and the screech of a gull had been the only noises on the journey across.

Cat's Eye Beach was dotted with brightly-coloured beach umbrellas. Couples walked hand-in-hand along the shorelines and children played at the edge of the water with beach balls and coloured buckets and spades.

Relaxation seeped into Tam's bones and she drew in a breath and then let out a big sigh; she was so looking forward to these couple of days.

Evie had pulled the sail down and they were now under motor; the channel was busy with water traffic as catamarans and yachts headed out on charters and a boatload of backpackers passed them.

A dozen young people waved madly at them as they sat on the edge of the deck of the big yacht. Wetsuits hung over the side of the old vessel; they were obviously heading out to the outer reef. Tam had seen them leaving from Hamilton Island and Airlie Beach every time she'd come over. They usually had casks of wine or boxes of cider tucked under their arms as they set out for their adventure, and on their return, they were sunburned, hungover and hungry.

Interesting, she thought as she tapped her lip with one finger.

They hadn't considered the backpacker market for the resort, as that age group was usually looking for cheaper accommodation, but it might be worth talking to the local operators on Hamo about going for that niche of the market. Tam's brain kicked into gear as she thought about the sorts of things they could do to cater for backpackers: they could do some glamping tents with an amenities block at the far end of the beach and offer kayaking and parasailing and more, so boats loaded with backpackers heading back from the reef sailing trips could stop in on the way back. She could set up a takeaway hamburger service. Orders could be phoned in and the boats could—

She pulled herself up with a smile. *I'm supposed to be having a break. From now on all I'll focus on is time out.*

She waved back to the backpackers and headed up to the front of the yacht to help Evie with the mooring.

'Thanks for asking me to come with you, Tam,' Evie said as Tam dropped the fenders over the side so the yacht didn't scrape the concrete wharf.

'My pleasure. I'm really happy you and Sienna came too. Things have got a bit intense on the island over the last couple of weeks. We're all getting worked up about the opening, I think.'

'I've noticed,' Evie said. 'Tempers have been a bit short. I keep out of it, but I have noticed the tension.'

'We've all worked pretty hard over the past couple of months, so I guess tension is a given. I've got to learn to hold my tongue. Pippa's the boss.'

'We have worked hard, but it's exciting. I'm

really grateful to Pippa and you and Nell for letting me be a part of this team.'

'You've fitted in really well.' Tam moved back to stand beside Evie at the helm. 'We are a team, but the resort is Pippa's.'

'Yeah, but you three are tight, that's why I sort of stay away a bit. I don't want to intrude on a friendship.'

'You don't need to worry about that. You're as much a part of the team as the rest of us. And now Eliza's back, and Sienna's here, please don't feel as though you're not part of us.

'Pippa and Nell and I have been friends since primary school, and we've had our ups and downs. We've spent a lot of time apart over the past few years with relationships—some good, some bad, and with our careers—again, some good, some not so good—and it's been great to get back together on the island. But I think if I'm honest it's got a little bit intense; we have to learn how to separate our friendship from our work environment.' Tam lowered her voice and glanced across at Sienna, but she was watching a yacht move into the berth beside them and wasn't listening. 'I've been intolerant and childish, so I can take some of the blame for the tension this week. I was flat out and Eliza swanned back, and I got a bit pissed off.'

'Why are you pissed with her?'

'They said when they came back that they had news, and there's been meetings up at Rafe's house, so I guess I'm a little bit peeved at not being in the loop. But that is really stupid because the bottom line is Pippa employs us to do a job and I'm the chef. I'm going to apologise to her and Pippa when we get back.'

'That's why I keep to myself,' Evie said. 'I don't want Pippa to think I am taking advantage of a past friendship. I owe her; she was there for me in a hard time of my life.'

'Our Pippa is a good person.' Tam put her arm around Evie's shoulder. 'Like I said I've been selfish and childish. We can all work together, and we can be workmates and friends. I guess the worry is, it's an unknown for us. We've all invested in the island—not financially for Nell and me, but with our hopes and dreams. If it doesn't work out, we'll have to go back to the real world and get real jobs. Nell and I anyway. Now that Pippa and Rafe are engaged, her future is on the island. Who knows how it will go with the way the tourism industry is going? The cyclone decimated the region a couple of years back and it's only just coming good now. I worry if we'll even get many guests the way the economy is.'

'But the huts are getting lots of bookings,' Evie said. 'Nell was telling me that yesterday.'

'Maybe curiosity at this stage? I just know that we must make it a spectacular opening on Friday night. Jiminy told Pippa there's a real buzz on Hamo about us opening, so local businesses might help us as well. And there's about a hundred booked for the opening.' Tam frowned. 'Shit, I hope I have enough food prepared. Maybe I shouldn't have taken these two days off. Pippa was probably right. Listen, Evie, remind me on the way back on Thursday to pick up some frozen spring rolls and things like that at the General Store. I hate the idea of serving pre-packaged food but if we run out, I don't want to be caught short.'

'By the time you run out of food—and I doubt

that you will—the guests will be so well lubricated they won't even notice. You've got to enjoy the night too. It's going to be a celebration for all of us.' Evie looked past Tam across to the wharf. 'I remember at my wedding my dad was so stressed about food running out, he didn't enjoy himself at all. He spent most of the night talking to the caterer.'

'I didn't realise you'd been married,' Tam said as Evie cut the engines. It's the first time Evie had volunteered any personal information and Tam was surprised.

'Yeah, past history. We learn from our mistakes.'

'I'll second that,' Tam said.

Evie didn't speak again until she had secured the ropes. 'I'll just go up to the marina office and pay for the berth.'

Tam watched as Evie hurried up to the concourse where the marina building overlooked the wharves. With her high ponytail poking through her baseball cap, and slim build she looked like a teenager, but Tam knew she was the same age as she and Pippa and Nell were. The big Three-O was coming up quickly for all of them. By the time Evie came back Tam just had enough time to check in to the room and get to the hairdresser.

'Message me via Facebook when you're back in your room and I'll bring the bubbles,' Evie said with a grin.

'Will do. After that, I thought we might just have an easy night tonight and try some finger foods at one of the bars, and then tomorrow night there's a restaurant I want to try, that is if you girls are happy with that.'

'Sounds good to me. I'll see you both later,' Evie said.

Tam nodded, and she and Sienna grabbed their bags and were soon heading along Resort Drive to the Reef Hotel where Tam had booked a twin room. 'We could grab one of the buggies if you don't want to walk with those bags,' she said to Sienna.

'It's fine, They're not heavy. I'm happy to walk through the streets and absorb the atmosphere. It's so different from home. When we got off the plane and met Rafe here the other day, we went straight to his boat, so I didn't get a chance to have a look around. I am loving it already.'

'There's a lot to do here: parasailing, kayaking, day trips. Not to mention all the coffee shops, and places to eat, some great bars and if you like clothes shopping the boutiques have some good stuff, but they're pricey.'

'I love your dress, Tam. Did you get it here?'

'No. I haven't been shopping since we left the Gold Coast. I don't need anything apart from my work clothes on the island. Besides, I love vintage shopping and the retro shop here is really exxie. Like thousands in some of the high-class boutiques for a dress or bag. This'—she gestured down to her favourite dress— 'is a nineteen-sixties dress I picked up at a retro shop in Brisbane for ten dollars.'

'I won't be doing much shopping here. I'm on a budget. As much as I love my work, my overheads are still really high,' Sienna said. 'I really appreciate you paying for the hotel room and I'm going to enjoy giving you and Evie your treatments. I might even see if they need a casual beautician in any of the day spas on "Hamo" as you call it. While I'm here, I might as well earn some money. Eliza paid my airfare. She wanted to see if I would be interested in moving here eventually. She was talking about a day spa on the island one day.'

'There's a lot of business discussion going on up at the house,' Tam said curiously. 'And yes, I know a day spa has been mentioned for our island once we get up and running.'

'That'd be great, but I'll have to go back before then. Between you and me, I think they might be talking about putting up some more huts.'

'Eliza built the first three.'

'I know and Eliza will tell you more, I'm sure, but she's in a different financial position since she went back to Italy; that's the only reason I accepted her kind offer of paying my airfare. That's all I'll say but you might understand the gist of what I'm saying.'

'Not my business.' Tam said with a shrug. 'It's Pippa's venture. We're just there to help. I'm looking forward to getting my restaurant open in the future. It'll be the first one where I'll be in charge.'

They turned the corner into the main shopping street and Sienna smiled as a group of good-looking young guys walked past them.

'Hmm. The locals aren't bad.'

'Not many locals here. It's the weather this time of the year that brings everyone here, and all winter too,' Tam said.

'Bit different to home,' Sienna said. 'It was snowing when I flew out of Zurich. I could live here. I'll have to find myself a millionaire.'

Tam laughed. 'Or a job.'

Chapter Six

Gabe

Gabe leaned back and reached for his coffee and was surprised to see the mug was empty.

Again.

He was onto his fourth coffee since he'd started, and he was buzzing. Although he'd been on the laptop for three hours, he had made little progress so far.

The woman he was seeking was the only suspect in the case. Gabe had been given the task of quietly checking her out and reporting back to Lukas Werner. Tamsin Jones was a common name; he'd found over a hundred women with that name already and most of them lived in Wales. Lukas had given him little information apart from she'd lived on the Gold Coast before she'd headed north to work on Pentecost Island—Lukas didn't even know what sort of work she was doing there—and that she was around thirty. By the time he'd applied filters to his search, he'd narrowed the set down to twenty-four

Tamsin Jones in Australia. He'd trawled the data on the first twenty-one so far and was worried that he was not going to have success.

If that was the case, he would have to go to the island blind, and get as much information as he could firsthand. His search was slowed by the fact that Lukas didn't have a photo of the target, so Gabe had to trawl through all the information for each of the names that he'd pulled up.

He knew better than to accept the age of a person from their Facebook photo; he'd learned that lesson in many of the cases he'd investigated over the past five years.

People liked to look good, and it was often hard to reconcile the profile photo on Facebook or Instagram with the real person. They didn't use a current one, and often they substituted someone else's photo. That had made some of his jobs very difficult a number of times. This time the search was more difficult because Lukas didn't have a photo of Tamsin Jones for him to compare. That would have made the process much faster.

Some possibilities had been slow to eliminate;

he'd found Facebook pages for twenty of them in Australia and been able to eliminate all the ones he'd checked so far by crossmatching their location with the years that he knew that Tamsin Jones had worked for his client's family on the Gold Coast.

If the general public knew how much of a footprint they left behind on social media, they'd think twice before they posted where they were going, and—he rolled his eyes—in some cases what they ate for each meal every day.

Gabe turned back to the laptop and scrolled down to the next Tamsin Jones. He sat up straight and nodded as he read the profile description on Facebook; Tamsin Jones, Chef Extraordinaire.

Don't get too excited; it might not be her, he warned himself.

He clicked on the profile and a happy face smiled back at him. This woman was the right age to fit the profile he was looking for, and he scrolled down to the "About" section.

Yes. He felt like cheering. He recognised the Gold Coast in some of the photos in her album even though she had no location listed.

Getting closer.

He clicked again and swore when the page came up blank.

Damn. The privacy settings were high, and he couldn't access any posts.

Smart lady, this one.

He clicked on her friends' list and nodded when it was blank too. Very smart user, she knew how to keep her settings private.

But Gabe was not easily deterred. He closed the screen and opened the dark web and set to work. Within minutes, he had the Facebook username and password for this Tamsin Jones. He switched back to Facebook, opened up a new screen and logged into her account. Satisfaction filled him as a photo of Pentecost Island appeared as her cover photo.

His search was over.

'Hello, Ms Tamsin Jones,' Gabe said quietly. 'I'm about to get to know you.'

In the small circle on the left was the same face that had come up in his previous search.

A pretty face framed by blonde curls and a stunning smile looked out at him. He wondered as he did in many of his cases why people gave into their dishonest inclinations. In some of his cases, he'd been able to understand their motivation, and although it was not his role to judge, it was hard not to sympathise with some. The case of the female bank teller who had taken ten thousand dollars to help pay for the medical treatment of her child with cancer had been hard to investigate, but it had had a good outcome when she wasn't charged.

So, he knew not to judge hastily. But sadly, in ninety percent of the cases he'd solved, the motivation had simply been greed.

'What's your story, Ms Jones?' he wondered aloud as he scrolled through her profile. 'Did you do it? And if you did, did you think you'd get away with it?'

Most of her posts included photos of an old house and shots of a beach, with little text and he assumed both were on the island he was about to visit.

Many of her likes and the posts that she had accessed were food related; that made sense seeing she was a chef.

Gabe spent about fifteen minutes on her page, before he realised there was nothing to be learned. As he was about to log out a notification popped up on the top right of the screen. She had a message from someone called Evie.

He had no hesitation in clicking on it.

Reef Hotel? What room? About to leave. Two bottles of bubbles enuff??? The message was followed by a smiley face.

God, he hated social media.

The reply was instant. **Room 232. Shake a leg. We've already opened a bottle and the face fun has started. Then we're going to the outdoor bar at the yacht club for sunset so bring your glam gear.**

Damn, he thought. She wasn't on Pentecost Island. Although the receptionist had said Tamsin Jones would be catering for the function on Friday night, so she should be there when he turned up.

He moved straight to Google and another smile crossed his face.

Reef Hotel? He was in luck.

His quarry was on Hamilton Island. Smack bang where he was.

It looked like he would be going to the local Yacht Club to watch the sunset.

As Gabe closed the laptop and headed for the shower, he wondered how investigators had worked before the advent of the internet and social media.

Chapter Seven

Tamsin

Tamsin sipped her champagne and chuckled as she looked in the mirror. 'Who is that woman?'

Evie picked up her glass and came to stand beside her. 'And who is this woman?'

'I think you're Evie,' Tamsin said.

'And I think you're Tamsin.' Evie chuckled too and they clinked glasses.

Sienna zipped up her makeup suitcase and came over to stand behind them. 'You were both a pleasure to work with.'

'Sienna, you are a magician. It doesn't even look like me!' Tam stared into the mirror. Her hair had been lightened with foils at the hairdresser and her curls were much fuller than usual with the product the hairdresser had added. Her eyes looked huge; Sienna had shadowed Tam's browbone with a gradient of different colours moving from beige to golden brown. Her lids were accentuated in a pale plum shade that matched her nail polish. Somehow, she had made her face look thinner and Tam's cheekbones appeared high and sharp. Her lips were outlined in a bright plum to match the flowers in the dress that she had decided to wear out tonight.

Evie's mouth was in a wide O. 'I have never looked like this in my life. How on earth do you do it? No wonder you look so gorgeous all the time, Sienna.'

Sienna came over and stood behind them. 'Tam, you create with food, Evie, you work with the soil and the air and water to create beautiful gardens. I get to work with beautiful faces and enhance what you don't see.'

'I'm not beautiful,' Tam said. 'And I'm not fishing for a compliment. My face is round and chubby, and my eyes are always too heavy-lidded. You've given me cheekbones, how on earth did you do that?'

Sienna's pretty laugh surrounded them. 'If I gave away my trade secrets, I wouldn't have a job. And you don't have a chubby face!'

'We're both ready to go. You go and get dressed, Sienna, or we'll miss our sunset.' Tam topped up their glasses as Sienna disappeared into her bedroom.

'A swish room,' Evie said as they walked out to the balcony.

'Yeah, I asked for a twin room, and when we came up, it was a two-bedroom apartment for the same price. If you want to crash here tonight, there's a spare bed in each room, and the sofa in the living room turns into a bed too. Safer than walking to the marina by yourself.'

Evie laughed. 'The yacht club is closer to the marina than the hotel.'

'Ah yes, but who knows where we'll end up. There's a few nightclubs up this way too.'

Sienna was out in a couple of minutes and Tam and Evie whistled. 'How do you do that so quickly!'

She linked her arms through theirs. 'Years of practice. Come on, girls, let's go watch this sunset. And then you can show me a good Aussie night on the town.'

##

Tam was radiant with excitement by the time they reached the yacht club. It might have been that there were three of them, or it might have been Sienna's skills, but they'd attracted one hell of a lot of attention.

Or it might have been the bubbles creating this happy feeling, but Tam was feeling pretty mellow. And the fact there were some good looking men out and about tonight didn't hurt either.

'I'm here for a good time, not a long time,' she said with a giggle, and the other two girls laughed.

The yacht club was busy, but they managed to get the last table in the outdoor bar.

'I'm going to grab us some food to soak up the bubbles we've already had. Any preferences?' Tam asked after they were settled at the table.

'You're the foodie,' Evie said. 'I'll go and get the drinks. Another bottle?'

'Why not?' Tam and Sienna said together.

Tam walked over to the bistro and perused the menu on the wall behind the counter.

Something substantial, she thought, if Evie's getting another bottle of champagne. They'd only shared one in the apartment, and they'd drunk that over a couple of hours.

'I can recommend the sea scallop platter,' a deep voice said beside her. 'It was so good I'm thinking of having another one.'

Tam turned and encountered a pair of dark eyes looking at her with interest.

'I hope I'm not being greedy,' he said.

'Well, on that recommendation, I'll have to try them. How many come on the platter?' she asked.

'Only three, sadly. So, I guess I'm not being greedy.'

'It all depends on your appetite, I guess,' she said holding his gaze.

'Oh, I have an excellent appetite.' He smiled back revealing a set of perfect white teeth as he flirted with her.

All the better to eat you with, Tam thought, and held back a giggle. This guy looked like he would appreciate sophistication. With the job Sienna had done of her face, and the new hair, she could do sophisticated.

'Are you with someone?' he asked.

'I am. You?'

'Alas, I am alone.' Tam didn't know if it was the deep voice or the sexy eyes that sent the butterflies into a frenzy in her belly. He was tall and broad, and his dark brown eyes matched his dark hair.

'It's too nice a night to be spending it alone. You're most welcome to join us. Just let me order.' She gave her order to the cashier and handed her card over. 'I'm Tamsin Jones.' Tam held out her hand.

He took her hand in his and Tam was gratified by the spark that flashed into his eyes as he took her hand.

'How do you do, Tamsin Jones.' His smile sent a warm shiver down her back. The night was improving by the second. 'I'm Gabe Brown and I'd love to join your group.'

***

Gabe

Gabe followed Tamsin to the table at the edge of the balcony. He waited for her to lead the way even though he knew where they were sitting outside. They had arrived at the club shortly after he had sat down at a table that had a clear view of the door.

He had almost missed their arrival because

Tamsin had been standing behind the other two women. It was the blonde curls that had caught his attention as they walked across the club to the outside balcony. Her Facebook photograph didn't do her justice; she was beautiful. Her dress hugged a curvaceous figure and he was sure she was unaware of the male interest that she attracted as she walked across to the door. The other two women she was with were attractive too, but his attention was on Tamsin.

How lucky was he that she was on the island, and he'd hooked up with her within an hour of finding her on Facebook?

She gestured to a stool and Gabe sat down, placing his beer on a coaster, aware of the surprise on the faces of the other two women.

'Evie, Sienna. This is Gabe. He's by himself so I invited him to join us.'

Gabe was savvy enough to know to share his attention around. He shook hands with both women.

'On holiday, Gabe?' The one with the shiny auburn hair asked. Her voice was slightly accented.

'A bit of both. Work and a holiday,' he

replied. 'What about all of you?'

'I'm on holiday. From Switzerland,' the woman called Sienna replied, 'but Tamsin and Evie work over on Pentecost Island where I am staying with my friend.'

'Sounds like a dream job, working up here on the islands,' he directed his comment to Tamsin.

'It is. Absolute paradise.' As Tamsin replied, she leaned forward to reach for her drink, and her leg brushed against his. The electric shock that ran upwards was not one that he'd expected . . . or wanted.

He was not here to succumb to her charms as his client's father had done. He had a task to complete, and he would do it. If it meant playing up to her, so be it. He kept that in the forefront of his mind as the casual conversation continued. Being able to encounter her in a social situation was a bonus. Now he had to win her trust.

Gabe kept his eyes on Tamsin as she explained what they were doing on the island. Her jewellery was understated; a fine gold chain around her neck and a simple gold ring on her left hand.

Nothing expensive or showy.

'My grandmother's wedding ring,' she said, and he quickly lifted his gaze. Gabe would have to learn to be less obvious. He reached over and pretended an interest in the ring. 'It has an unusual pattern in it. It looks quite modern.'

'You know your jewellery?' she asked curiously.

'No. The pattern caught my eye. It looks Egyptian.'

'That's not modern.' Tamsin frowned and lifted her hand to catch her ring with the last of the light. The sun was a golden ball in the west and would shortly disappear behind the mountains on the mainland. 'Do you think so? I've never noticed.'

It was an excuse to reach over and take her hand, and again he wasn't prepared for that jolt of electricity that ran up his fingers. He peered at the ring, her fingers warm against his.

'No, I was wrong. It looks like initials wound together at a closer look.'

As she leaned over, Tamsin's leg pressed against his thigh and stayed there. Gabe smiled with satisfaction. Excellent, she was taking the bait.

'So, tell me what you do on the island?' he asked. 'And of more interest to me, how long are you on Hamilton Island?'

Her head was close to his. The other two women were talking to each other.

'I'm the chef,' she said softly. 'We haven't opened yet, and we're taking a break over here before our official bar opening on Friday night. Just two days and two nights.'

'Sweet. I'm here by myself and I'd appreciate some company. Would you join me for a coffee tomorrow morning?' He kept his voice low as the others talked.

Tamsin looked up and held his gaze steadily. 'Me? Or all of us?'

He smiled and moved his head closer to hers. Her hair smelled sweet. 'You're quick on the uptake. You, Tamsin. I'd really enjoy getting to know you better.'

'Coffee would be good. But tell me why you're on the island? You said work and a holiday? What sort of work do you do, and how long are you staying?'

He forced a sigh. 'I'd love to say it's mainly a holiday, but I'm here for work.' He used his usual cover story. 'I'm in IT.' It was close enough to the truth that he never got caught out in casual conversations.

'That's interesting. One of our friends—and part-time barman at our resort is in IT. He has a lot of business contracts on Hamo. I wonder if you know him.'

Shit, Gabe thought.

'What's his name?

'Nat Dwyer. He was at uni with us in Brisbane and his partner, Nell, manages the resort.'

Gabe shook his head. 'No. I don't recognise the name, but this is my first trip to the islands. I'm doing a bit of leg work to see if it's worthwhile advertising up here.'

She looked at him curiously. 'What sort of IT work?'

Damn, but she was on the ball.

'You could say I'm a jack of all trades. A bit of everything. But enough about me. Tell me how you came to the islands. Have you always been a chef?'

'I started off doing Arts at uni but didn't last long before I took up a traineeship at Peppers at the Gold Coast. I think that's what I always wanted to do, but my dad wanted me to go to uni. I didn't last, and he was happy that I followed my dream in the end. And how we came to Pentecost Island? It's a good story actually. Pippa was left the island by a relative. We were all at a bit of a loose end, and our skills fitted with what she was looking for. . . so here we are. Why don't you come across to the island to our function on Friday night?'

'Is it invitation only?'

'No, we're taking bookings, but if you would like to come'—her look was coy— 'I'll book you in.'

'I'll let you know before you go back.'

The last thing he wanted was for her to find out that he'd already booked the opening, and accommodation in one of the huts a week later. Gabe knew he should have been upfront about his booking in the first place and treated it as a coincidence, but he thought he might find out more about her by playing dumb. So far, he'd discovered nothing he hadn't already known. And she hadn't mentioned her time working for the Werners.

That was interesting.

'We've been working hard all winter to get the place ready, and I'm proud to say we've done most if it ourselves.' She gestured around to the bar. 'Nowhere near as sophisticated as this sort of bar, but I think we're going to have more atmosphere. After all, it's all about location, isn't it?'

'Location, location,' he agreed holding her gaze. He was pleased to see a little bit of pink tinge on her cheeks.

The waitress brought the food to the table, and Gabe knew that he'd lost Tamsin's attention as she looked at the trays holding a variety of finger food. He almost rolled his eyes when she pulled out her phone and snapped some photos of the plates.

He waited until she was finished, but she turned and gestured to the tray before he could speak again.

'Have one,' she said pointing at the scallops. 'You forgot to order yours.'

He leaned closer. 'I was too busy looking at you,' he said with a smile. 'You're a very beautiful woman, Tamsin.'

Her laugh was rueful, but she didn't move away. 'This isn't the real me. I've been pampered today. Hairdresser, and nails and facial by the lovely Sienna.'

'Mm, Pampering sounds good.'

'There should be more of it.' She held his gaze steadily, and her hand reached out and touched his thigh.

He was barely able to control his reaction and pulled his thoughts away from the beautiful woman beside him and tried to focus on why he was here. After a moment, he looked away and caught the knowing glance that the other two exchanged.

'I'll leave you to enjoy your night out, but I would love to have that coffee with you tomorrow, Tamsin?'

'Sure. I think the girls will be hitting the shops, won't you?'

They both nodded very quickly, but Sienna's eyes were strangely wary. 'We sure will be.'

'Can I pick you up at your hotel?'

'That would be good.'

'Say ten?'

'I'll see you then.'

'I'll look forward to it,' Gabe said. 'Have a good evening, ladies.'

His smile was for Tamsin alone before he turned and walked out of the bar.

Chapter Eight

Tamsin

When Gabe was out of sight Evie put a hand to her chest. 'Oh, be still my beating heart. What a honey.'

Sienna frowned. 'He was smitten with you, Tam. It was a bit quick.'

'Nah, he was just being friendly. He seems like a nice guy.' Tam smiled at them, feeling good.

'He was smitten. I saw the way he was looking at you at the counter before he spoke to you. He stared and stared at you for about five minutes while you were looking at the board.' Sienna said.

'Well, maybe. While you were chatting, he asked me out for coffee tomorrow. I said yes, but would you girls mind? Maybe you wanted us to go on a cruise or parasailing or something.'

Evie shook her head. 'I'm happy to chill on the beach. No physical activity for me. I'm here to have a rest.'

'Me either,' Sienna chipped in. 'Beach for me. We don't have any in Switzerland. So, go have your coffee and then we can go out for lunch together.'

Evie chuckled. 'Unless you want some . . .um . . . physical activity, Tam?'

'Are you being smart, Miss Evie?' Tam raised her eyebrows.

'Who me?' Evie's face was a picture of innocence. 'I thought you might want to go kayaking or something?'

Tam grinned. 'Well, I did tell Nell I was looking for a good time while I was here.'

'Call it what you like,' Sienna said. 'I think Mr Good Looking Gabe was interested in having "a good time". You be careful.'

'And he's not a sleaze either,' Evie said. 'He was considerate enough not to muscle in on what was obviously a girls' night out. I say go for it, Tam!'

'Ha, wait until he sees me tomorrow without the soft evening light and the face paint. He might run a mile.'

'You're gorgeous without the face paint.' Sienna wagged a finger. 'It's all in the confidence, you know. Know that you are beautiful inside and out, and you will exude that confidence. That was the first thing we were taught at beauty school. It's a good rule to follow.'

Tam laughed and waved her hand. 'We'll see if he turns up or not.' She bit her lip. 'Damn, he won't you know! I didn't tell him where we were staying.'

'You were both too much into the gooey eyes,' Evie said.

'Gooey eyes?' Sienna burst out laughing. 'Please tell me what are gooey eyes? I've never heard of them before.'

Evie giggled. 'You know when two people make moon eyes at each other.'

Sienna joined in with a snort, and Tam couldn't help laughing back. She was getting to love these girls' company.

'At home we call them cow eyes,' Sienna said.

'Stop it, you pair. I probably won't see him again, but it was fun flirting and he told me about these wonderful scallops.' Tam pointed to the last one on the plate. 'I'll fight you for it.'

'It's all yours, love,' Evie said.

Sienna nudged Evie. 'Doesn't the saying go,

the way to a *man's* heart is through his stomach? Gabe got it back to front.'

Evie's grin was wicked. 'I think he got it right. Anything to do with food is a pickup line for Tam.'

'Hey, leave me alone, you pair. Food is my profession, and these are yum. I think I know what's in the sauce. I'll get some frozen scallops at the store and give the sauce a go when we get home.' She licked her fingers. 'It's an occupational hazard, tasting food. That's why I have a weight problem.'

'Tam, you listen to me.' Sienna's finger was wagging again. 'You do not have a problem with your weight. You are perfect just as you are. You look healthy and glowing. And that was before the makeup too!'

Evie was astute. 'Is your perception of your body image—and I agree with Sienna, you don't have a problem—because someone once said you had a weight problem?'

Tam stared past them to the sky that was turning apricot as the sun sank towards the mountains. The water was dark purple, and mast lights were beginning to appear on the water. It was a beautiful evening, and the warm breeze carried a hint of spice. She turned back to the girls. 'You're spot on, Evie. It's amazing how one criticism can stay with you for a long time, isn't it? The moral of the story? Don't ever go out with a fitness fanatic. I was in a relationship, and all he wanted to do was drag me out of bed to the gym at some ungodly hour every morning, even after we'd worked until midnight in the restaurant. I was more interested in being in bed with him than on sweaty machines, and when I protested, he told me if I didn't look after myself, I would be even fatter before I was thirty.'

'I hope you ditched him.'

Tam sniffed. 'No, he ditched me for someone from the gym.'

'How long were you together?'

'About a year. I was all ready for the engagement ring and the fancy wedding, and the house and kids' route. He wanted a skinny chick with plastic boobs. A great escape for me, hey?' Tam kept her voice bright; there was a lot more to the Chad story, but she never shared that with anyone. 'What about you, Sienna? Any long-lost lovers pining for you back home?'

Sienna pointed to the almost empty bottle. 'Before I tell you my boring life story, I think we should get another bottle of bubbles. What do you think?'

'What do I think?' Tam said as she stood and poured the last of the bubbles into Evie and Sienna's glasses. 'I think that is a definite yes. I knew you were both going to be great company. Shame we've only got two nights!'

##

Five hours later, Sienna and Tam stood at the top of the marina concourse and watched that Evie got safely back to her boat. They walked across the island back to the hotel, arm in arm.

'I've had the best night, Tam.' Sienna yawned as they reached the hotel. 'Do we want a nightcap in the bar?'

'I could go a coffee,' Tam said. They'd gone easy on the drinks all night and had dined in the restaurant at the yacht club, before ending up on the dance floor afterwards. 'I am going to be so sore tomorrow. I haven't danced like that since uni.'

'I haven't had so much fun since Eliza and I used to sneak out of our boarding school and go to dances at the village pub.' She grinned. 'Let's have a coffee.'

They sat on the soft sofas overlooking the pool adjacent to reception.

'It was a fun night,' Tam said.

'It was.' Sienna put her coffee cup back in the saucer and leaned forward with her elbow on her knee. 'Tam, can I say something?'

'Sure.' Tam was surprised when Sienna frowned. She thought she'd been going to ask about working at the resort and maybe ask Tam to put in a good word for her.

'Be careful tomorrow.'

'Tomorrow?' It was Tam's turn to frown. 'What do you mean be careful? I'm only having coffee and it will be in broad daylight. I guess that's what you meant. Gabe?'

'Just coffee then. Don't go running off with him.'

Tam laughed and then stopped when she saw Sienna's face.

'You know Eliza's story, don't you?' she said quietly.

'I know she had a pretty nasty marriage.'

'Did you know we were on holiday together when she met Rocco?'

'No, I didn't know that.'

'I blamed myself for not seeing what he was like. When she disappeared and then we heard she had died, I had a breakdown. I ended up in a facility in Switzerland for a month. I've never told Eliza that. But it all came back tonight.'

'I won't say anything, but I'm pleased you trusted me enough to share that. You seem to be very good friends.'

'Eliza and I have the same sort of friendship that you have with Nell and Pippa. I haven't seen a lot of you together in the short time I have been on the island, but Eliza told me all about you three and how you have been friends since school.'

'We have been, and we all know each other well. So well, that I worry about Pippa and Rafe coming unstuck. I've had bad experiences'—for a moment Tam was tempted to share but decided not to— 'and Nell's done it tough. You have no need to worry about me tomorrow. I will never give my heart to a man again, and trust me, Sienna, I am very, very wary.'

'I'm pleased to hear that. But if you're not back by noon, I'll come looking.'

Tam did laugh then. 'You're a dill, Sienna but a lovely one. I appreciate your concern but trust me, I'm a big girl and I know how to look after myself.'

Chapter Nine

Gabe

Gabe woke up the next morning with something niggling at him, but he couldn't put a finger on it. He'd gone straight back to the apartment when he'd left the yacht club last night and spent a few hours online with a limited amount of success before he called it a night.

After browsing through Tamsin's friends on Facebook and Instagram, and looking at their posts, he'd learned a little bit more about her.

She had been tagged in a number of posts, and some of the privacy settings of her friend's pages were non-existent. He found out more about her there than he had from her profile.

Ten years of posts, and photographs of her at various weddings and social occasions. He tracked one friend and in a deep Google search, he came across some photographs of Tamsin at an awards ceremony for the prestigious Chef of the Year competition in Brisbane three years ago. She was obviously an excellent chef; she'd been a finalist in the competition.

Confused, he picked up the phone and dialled Lukas Werner in Melbourne.

'Gabe.' Lukas answered immediately. 'Do you have news for me? Have you found it?'

'No, not yet, but I wanted to check some information with you. Are you sure that the Tamsin Jones who worked for your parents is the one who is up here in the islands?'

'Yes. it's her. No doubt.'

'Why did your parents employ her? How did she get the job?'

'I can't answer that. They didn't ever say. I came back from an overseas trip, and the previous assistant had left, and she was working there.'

'So she worked there for about eighteen months and finished up early this year when they sold the shop?'

'No. I might not have been clear enough before. They didn't sell, they closed it. Their sort of personalised store was an anachronism in the current retail market. There was too much competition from the chain store jewellery lines; they simply couldn't compete.'

'And tell me again when you noticed the ring was missing?'

'Dad asked me to do a stock inventory before they put the precious pieces into the bank security vault. They cleared much of the stock, but there was a lot that didn't sell. Most of it very valuable. I talked him out of keeping it in the safe at home. Every time I went over there it wasn't even locked. Mum likes to wear the expensive pieces and couldn't see why I was worried.

'Where they live on the Gold Coast, break and enters are rife, and I knew it was only a matter of time before it happened to them. The word would soon get around that they had a fortune in jewellery in their safe.'

'And you're one hundred percent sure that Tamsin Jones was the name of the woman who worked for them, and she now lives in the Whitsunday Islands?'

'Yes, she still keeps in touch with Mum; she sent her a birthday card last month and told her about a new resort she's working at.'

'Did she say what sort of work?'

'No, but I imagine she'd have been a retail assistant. She didn't have any qualifications to my knowledge. Or there weren't any in her employment file.'

'Thanks, mate. If you can chase up a photo from your parents that would be a great help. I'll be in touch in a few days. I'm on the trail.'

And he was. What he couldn't understand was why a top-class chef would go and work in a jewellery store as a shop assistant, and not divulge her qualifications and past, especially when she had been so highly regarded in the industry. There was another mystery there.

Gabe's sleep was full of dreams about a blonde woman, but even though he knew it was Tamsin, he couldn't see her face. They were swimming together in crystal clear water, and she kept trying to entice him out to the deep water where she was swimming. So simplistically symbolic, even he could interpret that dream.

He'd broken his first rule; he was attracted to his quarry. Gabe woke feeling unsettled and he went back to his laptop to see if she'd posted anything overnight or had any messages.

Usually, it didn't bother him, but he felt as though he was intruding on her privacy.

Shit, she had already got herself into his head. Or into his emotions, he admitted to himself. He had been very attracted to Tamsin Jones, and that had never happened to him before in an investigation.

He had spent an hour with her, and already he couldn't get her face out of his head.

##

Gabe was waiting outside the Reef Hotel at five minutes before ten and as soon as he saw the surprise on her face when Tamsin walked into the foyer, he knew what had been niggling at him.

Jeez, mate. A great PI you are. He hadn't asked her where she was staying. He knew where she was staying from reading her messages. Quickly, he covered his tracks.

'Great guess,' Gabe said with a wide smile. 'I felt like an idiot when I realised I didn't know where you were staying, so I started at the biggest hotel and if you hadn't appeared, I was going to go to all the coffee shops and eliminate them one by one. I wasn't going to stand you up even if it took all day!'

'You've done good. I realised when you left that I hadn't told you and I didn't know where you were staying, so I was going to do the same. Try all the coffee shops!'

'Shall we go find one?' Gabe crooked his elbow and was pleased when Tamsin slid her hand through his. 'Or how about here? I walked past one near the pool on the way in.'

'Let's go further afield. The girls are in the pool. And I feel like a walk in the fresh air. As much as I like the luxury, a hotel room can get claustrophobic very quickly. Where are you staying?'

'I've got an apartment up the hill from the shops. Great views, big rooms and an infinity pool.'

'How long did you say you were staying?'

'I've booked it for a week. But I might stay up in the islands longer. It's better than Melbourne.'

Her hand was warm against his skin as they walked through the shade of the large trees that shaded the entrance to the hotel.

'Melbourne. Would you believe I've never

been there?'

'At the moment you're not missing anything. It's cold and bleak, and waiting for spring to arrive.'

Tamsin turned her head to face him as they walked down the hill to the shopping area. 'I'm going to be upfront here, Gabe. When you go home is there anyone waiting for you? I don't like to step in on anyone else's territory.'

He squeezed her fingers. 'You can step in my territory any time, Tamsin.'

She stared at him and her clear gaze made *him* feel guilty.

'That's not what I asked. Wife? Girlfriend? Partner? Speak now or I'll assume there is.' She stopped walking and pulled her arm from his

Gabe shook his head. 'Does a mangy orange cat count? Owned by my eighty-year-old neighbour, but who seems to have adopted me.' He returned her gaze steadily and guilt pinged in his chest.

Her eyes were locked on his and she nodded. 'Good.' Her arm went back where it had been. 'Now we've got that out of the way, what are your plans for the day?'

'Is that an offer of your company?'

'No, I'm spending the rest of the day around the pool with the girls. We came here to have a break before we get into serious work. Well, Evie and I anyway, that is.'

He put on a mock pout. 'Dumped before I was even in your life.'

Why the hell did he say that. *In her life?*

Tamsin looked at him curiously. 'I was wondering if you'd like to have dinner with me tonight. I want to try one of the restaurants here, and the girls aren't keen. I'd prefer to have company.'

'I'd be delighted to take you to dinner.'

'Nope. We pay our own way.'

'Okay, I would be delighted to go to dinner with you.' Gabe frowned as they walked along. It was too easy to forget this was a job; he was enjoying her company way too much. 'Which restaurant is it?'

'It's called Stonehaven. It's in a gated community and you have to have a reservation. It's a six-course tasting menu with all wines included. I've already booked for two.' This time her look was coquettish.

'Ah, so you were sure of me, were you, Tamsin Jones?'

She shrugged as they walked along. 'If you'd said no, I would have found someone else.'

'Ah, I'm wounded.' Gabe put his hand to his chest.

'Why do you call me Tamsin Jones?'

'I like the sound of it. Your name has character.'

'Jones? I don't think so. It's as bad as Smith and Brown.' She put her hand over her mouth and giggled. 'Woops, I forgot. I really didn't mean that. Seriously though, how many times have people looked at you as though you're giving them a false name.'

Bloody hell. Gabe could feel the heat running up his neck, and then suspicion kicked in. Hang on a minute. Had she somehow found out that Brown was a false name and she was testing him out?

What to do? His mind raced.

Will I be honest? Should he say it's a business name? Or will that make her run?

Before he replied her hand tugged at his. 'I'm

sorry. Have I offended you? There is nothing wrong with being a Brown.'

'Of course not. Or a Jones. We have an advantage, people don't forget our names, and they never have trouble spelling them.'

Her laugh peeled out. 'That's true. I've never been asked how to spell Jones. Now Tamsin is a different matter. I've seen about six variations of the spelling, including Damson, which is a plum! And what about Gabe? Is that short for—?'

'Gabe. Just Gabe. Named after my grandfather.'

That was the first truthful thing he'd said to her this morning apart from Mrs Hamlin's mangy orange cat.

'And yes, it gets misspelled too.' Somehow her fingers had slid down his arm and were now entangled with his. It felt right. It felt good.

They walked along the main shopping precinct and passed a couple of coffee shops.

'Here?' he asked when they stood outside the first one.

Tamsin peered into the window and wrinkled

her nose. 'No. Not that one. There's another one about three shops down.'

There was, but it was packed too.

'How about a takeaway coffee?' Gabe suggested. 'We can walk down and look at the water. Or we could walk up to One Tree Hill and get a coffee there and look at the view.'

'Great idea. I'd forgotten there's a coffee shop up there. We can sit on the deck. There's a fabulous view from up there. You said this is your first visit. How did you know about that coffee shop?'

'The apartment I'm staying in isn't far from there. I've already sampled their coffee.'

'Good?'

'Very. And yes, the view is excellent too.'

Gabe was torn between looking at the woman sitting across the table from him or looking across the sapphire waters to the huge emerald-green island to the north.

'You look a bit overwhelmed,' Tamsin said as he stared out over the water.

'The colours here are incredible. The sky and the water.'

'I know, I'll never take it for granted. I have to pinch myself sometimes to realise this is home.' She tipped her head to the side and her eyes sparkled. 'I was just thinking yesterday I'll probably still be here when I'm old. I don't think I could ever leave.'

He shifted his attention back to Tamsin. 'That's a big decision to make at what? Twenty-four?' He was testing her honesty.

'Thank you. How about almost the big Three-O looming? What about you?' Her head went back to the side and she pursed her lips. 'I would say thirty-four.'

'Not a bad guess,' he said with a grin.

'So, I was right?' She looked up as the waitress brought their coffee and cake to the table. 'Thank you.'

'Not going to say.'

She was spot on. Damn it, he was really enjoying spending time with this woman, and he had to keep reminding himself this was a job. She was the sole reason he was up in the islands, and there was a hundred-thousand-dollar piece of jewellery to be found. Why couldn't she be a nasty shrew? His instincts never let him down—or they hadn't yet—and Lukas swore that Tamsin Jones was the guilty party.

'Want to share?'

Tamsin picked up her spoon and dug it into the pale orange cream beside the cake on her plate. His eyes followed the spoon as it went to her mouth and the tip of her tongue appeared between those pretty lips. She slowly licked the cream off the spoon. Gabe took a deep breath; he couldn't look away. How the hell was he going to sit opposite her at a dinner table for a six-course meal?

'Wow, that is so different.'

'What flavour is it?'

'I think it's mandarin and lemon mixed, and maybe a touch of honey. Really unusual on ginger cake.'

'You really appreciate your food, don't you?'

'I do. I love creating. And I love going out and trying other people's creations. Do you cook?'

'Um, I can make coffee. I have a machine.'

'What do you eat?' Her nose was screwed up in disbelief and it was cute.

'Whatever I fancy. I live near a restaurant street in Melbourne, and I can pick and choose every night.'

'Well, I can't wait until dinner tonight.'

'Ah, so you are looking forward to my company?' he teased.

'That too,' Tamsin said. She put the spoon down and looked at him. 'I'm enjoying your company. I'm pleased we met at the yacht club last night. You should have stayed. We danced for hours.'

'Dancing? I can't remember the last time I danced.'

'Me either, and I was sure I'd be sore this morning but I must be fitter than I thought. I don't get much time to exercise.'

'What about during the day? Don't chefs work mainly at night? Or am I assuming too much? Have you always been a chef?'

'I always wanted to be. And I got there in the end. A bit of a bumpy road along the way, but I don't like to dwell on the past.' Before he could ask more, she turned the conversation around. 'What about you? Were you always in IT?'

'Like you, a bit of a bumpy road on the way, but yes, I got there in the end.'

'Sounds like we have a bit in common. Apart from our love of scallops. I wonder if they'll be on the menu tonight.'

And the opportunity to keep the questions going was gone as Tamsin deftly switched the conversation back to food.

Chapter Ten

Tamsin

As Tamsin and Gabe walked out of the coffee shop, a shuttle bus came up the hill and turned into the coffee shop car park.

Once it was parked, Tamsin waved and called out to the driver. 'Jiminy!'

Gabe was not far behind her when she turned around. 'Gabe, come and meet my friend.'

The doors of the bus opened, and Tamsin stood back as three couples exited and headed across to the coffee shop. She moved forward and stood on the bottom step. 'Hey, Jim, what are you doing driving buses?'

'Hello, Tam. I'm filling in for my mate just for today. He had to go to Airlie, and I had no charters on, so I offered to do his shuttle runs.'

'Jiminy, this is my friend, Gabe.'

Tam stood back and Gabe reached in and shook hands with Jiminy.

'Good to meet you, mate. Any friend of Tam's and all that,' Jiminy said. 'Just over for the day,

Tam?"

'No, I'm taking a couple of days break with two of the girls. We're staying at the Reef Hotel.'

'I'm heading down that way now. Have you finished up here? Want a lift back?'

Gabe took her arm. 'That's a good idea, Tamsin, I have some work to do.' He looked across to Jiminy. 'Does the shuttle bus run from the hotel to Stonehaven tonight?'

'Sure does, mate. I'll be doing the pickups and drop offs later.'

'What time is our table booked for, Tamsin?' Gabe asked.

'Seven,' she said. 'I was going to meet you there, seeing as your apartment is up this way.'

'No. I'll meet you at your hotel and we'll get the shuttle up together, and then I'll see you home.'

'You don't have to, but thank you. You're a gentleman.' She couldn't help reaching over and touching his hand before she got on the bus. 'I'll see you tonight. Oh, and Gabe,' she called through the window as Jiminy started the bus, 'it's dressy too.'

Once the bus had started down the hill, Tam

couldn't help looking back at Gabe. He was a nice guy, and she knew she was too interested in him. He was standing there looking at the bus with the strangest expression on his face. As she watched, he turned, and his stance seemed almost dejected as he headed along the road.

'Got yourself a fella, Tam?' Jiminy grinned as he changed back a gear to go down the steep hill.

'Maybe.' She smiled back at him. 'Who knows.'

***

Later that afternoon back in the room, after lunch and a long sunbake by the pool, Tam put her head back and closed her eyes as Sienna worked her magic. She'd got Jiminy to drop her off at the shops on the way back to the hotel and had bought herself the most gorgeous dress.

And shoes.

And earrings

And a new bag.

'I haven't spent any money since I came up here,' she justified to herself as she handed over her credit card.

Ouch, that would put a hole in her bank balance.

'What do you think is the main colour in the dress, Evie? Blue or green?' Sienna looked at Tam's dress hanging on the front of the wardrobe door. Evie had come up to have a predinner drink with them before Tam went out, and then she and Sienna were having a pizza and movie night in the room.

'A real girls' chill out,' Evie said. 'I'm exhausted from lying around the pool all day.'

'Your eyes should be,' Sienna said drily. 'You should have seen her, Tam. She didn't take her eyes off the pool boy once all morning. He was gone by the time you arrived, but he was a cutie.'

'No harm in looking,' Evie said with a chuckle as she walked over to the dress.

'Are you sure you don't want to come to the restaurant?' Tam asked them for the tenth time.

'Are you nervous about going on a date, *cherie?*' Sienna asked as she rubbed moisturiser into Tam's face.

'No.' Tam swallowed.

'I think blue,' Evie finally replied. 'It's a

stunning dress, Tam.'

'It's a local designer and she does her own fabric. The colours reflect the reef landscape. The pattern on this fabric is the same shape as Heart Reef, she told me.'

'Okay, I'll do your makeup in blue tones. I wasn't sure if it was closer to green or blue,' Sienna rummaged in her makeup case.

'Definitely blue,' Evie said as she went over to the small fridge and pulled out a bottle of bubbles.

'Just a half a glass for me, thanks, Evie. There are about three different wines with the meal tonight.' Tam hesitated and then casually added. 'I'm not sure when I'll be home.'

Evie smiled. 'As in tonight or tomorrow morning?'

Tam nodded. 'I'll see what the night brings.'

'You just stay safe,' Sienna lectured with a frown.

'Yes, Mum. I have an out if I decide not to stay. Jiminy's driving the shuttle bus tonight.' She kept her eyes closed as Sienna worked her magic. 'But I'm pretty keen, Gabe's a nice guy, but who knows, he might not even have the same idea as me.'

Sienna and Evie burst out laughing.

'Trust me, love. I am sure he is on the same wavelength as you.'

Half an hour later, Tam slipped the dress over her head. It whispered against her bare skin, luckily, she'd thrown in a good set of bra and undies when she'd packed. The cotton sports bra and knickers that she usually wore wouldn't have done it justice. She took care to keep the dress away from her hair. Once her makeup was done, Evie had insisted on putting it up in a sort of French roll, with a few tendrils of curls hanging around Tam's face.

'You're good, Evie.'

'I was a hairdresser in a past life. I haven't lost my skills, but I still prefer working outside than being in a smelly salon all day.'

Tam walked out of her room. The two girls were sitting on the balcony with a glass in hand. Evie let out a shrill wolf whistle and Sienna put one hand to her chest with a sigh.

'Oh, Tam. You look so beautiful.'

'Thank you. It's a lovely dress. I'm really

pleased I gave in and bought it.' She looked down and smoothed her hands against the silky fabric. 'It's not too tight, is it?'

'No, it's perfect.' Sienna said.

'It's really different to your usual style, but it suits you very well.' Evie jumped up. 'I'll take a photo and text Nell and Pippa.'

'And then one of the three of us,' Tam insisted. 'A memory of our little holiday.'

The two girls joined her at the railing after Sienna had taken a photo of Tamsin with the water and palm trees behind her.

The photos were sent off to Pentecost Island, and there were two replies within seconds.

Pippa's was her usual dry tone: **I hope Evie and Sienna are going to dress up too. Shorts and T-shirts won't be allowed in our restaurant. Lookin' good, Tam.**

Tam burst out laughing when she read Nell's reply.

'Looks like you're having a good time.'

'I hope so, Nellie,' she said to herself. 'I do hope so.'

And the best part was, Gabe was thinking about coming over to Pentecost Island on Friday for the opening of Turtle Bar. Tam guessed that would hinge on tonight. Maybe after a night in her company he wouldn't want to spend any more time with her.

***

Jiminy picked him up at the apartment and Gabe stared through the window of the shuttle bus as it came down the hill. It was almost dark, and the island was coming alive as the restaurants and bars opened for the night. As they'd driven past the yacht club, he'd looked across at the marina. It looked like a fairyland of little houses in rows, but he knew they were sleek yachts and catamarans. Crowds were milling in the street as tourists headed out for a night of entertainment and dining.

Jiminy drew the bus to a stop in the roundabout at the entrance to the Reef Hotel. 'We don't leave here for twenty minutes. I've got a full busload getting on at this stop. Then we'll head straight up to Stonehaven. So, if you want to have a drink with Tam in the bar, you've got time. Better than sitting cramped up on a bus waiting to leave.'

'Thanks, we might do that. We're a bit early. Tamsin may not be down yet.' Gabe glanced at his watch before he made his way off the bus. 'See you in fifteen or so.'

Soft music and muted conversation met him as he walked through the tiled foyer of the hotel. There was a sweet smell pervading the air, and he looked across at the large arrangements of fresh lilies that filled two big containers at the entrance to the bar. He stepped into the bar and looked around but there was no sign of Tamsin yet.

He walked back out to the foyer and moved across to the double sofa and sat down. Within seconds the elevator pinged, and the doors opened.

Gabe caught his breath as Tamsin stepped out and looked around. She looked stunning—a vision in blue, she seemed taller, and the dress she wore hugged her body like a second skin.

He stood and walked across and took her hand before he leaned over and brushed his lips across her cheek.

'You look—' He shook his head and let his gaze travel from her elegant hairstyle, down past the figure-hugging dress, and to long bare legs and high blue shoes. 'Words fail me, Tamsin Jones. But if I was a man of words, it would be a word that conveyed indescribably beautiful.'

Her cheeks coloured pink and she smiled. 'Thank you. I went shopping. I figured Stonehaven is going to be pretty classy. And none of my dresses were really suitable.'

Gabe was pleased he'd worn his suit. He held out his arm. 'Jiminy said we have time for a quick drink before the shuttle leaves. Shall we?'

As Tamsin lifted her right hand Gabe caught the quick flash of a ring, but she slipped her hand through the crook of his elbow before he could get a good look. A hint of musky perfume drifted over when she moved closer. His heart was beating fast, and it wasn't all from the quick glimpse of that diamond ring.

Heads turned as they walked into the bar. Gabe was tall, well over six feet, and with Tamsin's high heels, and her hair piled high on her head, she was not much below him.

In his dark suit and her stunning blue dress, he

knew that made an impressive-looking couple.

Shame it wasn't for real.

Chapter Eleven

Tamsin

Gabe was quiet on the bus on the way up the hill to the restaurant, but it may have been because of the excited chatter as the passengers looked forward to their evening of degustation.

Excitement filled Tam too; her fingers tingled with anticipation and a warm feeling settled in her chest. She hadn't felt this happy for a long time. It was a different sort of happiness to what she took from her work. This was personal satisfaction and happiness, and the possibility of getting to know Gabe better tonight added to it. Not that she was looking for the same sort of relationship that Pippa and Nell had found themselves in recently—and suddenly. A 'friends with benefits' sort of relationship would suit Tam just fine. That was, if her first impressions of Gabe Brown were right, and of course, if he felt the same way.

But she was getting ahead of herself. She was here for the food experience; if nothing else came of the night it wouldn't matter. Tam was looking forward to seeing the exclusive restaurant, and the sampling the food. Sharing the occasion with an interesting—not to mention very good looking—man made it even better.

The wheels crunched on the gravel as the bus pulled into the Stonehaven car park.

'I'll be back at eleven to collect those who need to get back down to hotels,' Jiminy said. 'Have a great evening.'

'Thanks, Jim,' Tam said as Gabe stood behind her in the bus aisle.

'If we're already gone when you get back, we'll be back at my apartment having a nightcap, and I'll get Tamsin home,' Gabe said. 'So, don't wait around for us.'

Tam's anticipation grew.

'Will do.' Jiminy winked at Tam and her face heated.

They were last to leave the bus and Tam looked around with pleasure. The entrance to the restaurant was lit with soft in-ground lighting, just enough to let you find your way safely into the building. The strains of piano music drifted across to them and this time Tam slipped her arm into Gabe's without being asked. He put his other hand on hers and squeezed her fingers.

Tam let out a soft sigh.

'Atmospheric,' he said quietly as they followed the group to the restaurant.

'It is.'

They were met at the door by a maître d' and asked for their booking name, before being led to a table in the corner overlooking the gardens.

They might not stretch to a maître d' in their restaurant when it was eventually open—she smiled, unless Rafe was willing— but Tam took note of every little thing that added to the atmosphere.

'You're in your element, aren't you?' Gabe said with a smile.

'Yep, I am. I love it. And the food is still to come.'

The candlelight flickered on his face, and for a moment his face was shadowed.

'I hope you don't mind being here. I sort of railroaded you into it, didn't I?' Tam reached for the water glass but before she could pick it up, Gabe caught her hand in his.

'Please let me dispel any doubt you may have, Tamsin. If I hadn't wanted to be here with you, I wouldn't be.' The light caught her ring and his gaze was intense as he stared at it. 'That's a beautiful ring. It could almost be an engagement ring, but you're wearing it on your right hand.'

She smiled and looked at the ring. 'It was a gift. From someone who was very kind to me when I needed a friend.'

'Sounds like a good friend. Can I intrude and ask if it was a man? Someone you might still have feelings for?'

'No. It wasn't a man. A very dear friend.' Tam pulled her hand back and held it up to the light, before dropping her hand to her lap. 'It certainly looks like the real thing, but it's only a simulated diamond.'

Their conversation was interrupted by the arrival of the waiter, who explained how the meal would be presented. He handed Gabe a wine list and asked him to peruse it. 'I shall return when you have had time to choose.'

Gabe's smile was wide when the waiter left, and he handed the wine list over without even opening it. 'You're the leader tonight. You choose what you think will go with the courses.'

***

Gabe watched as Tamsin cast her eyes over the wine list. Her mouth dropped open slightly as she looked at the selection. He sat back and took pleasure in watching the expressions play over her face.

As much as he decided that he was going to treat this as an opportunity to find out more about her and find out how she had the ring in her possession, his emotions and his desire overtook that intention.

If she came back to his place and stayed the night, he should be able to photograph the ring while she slept. He pushed away the guilt that came with the motivation behind his intent. The main reason he wanted Tamsin to come back to his place was because he wanted her in his bed. At this moment the ring had nothing to do with wanting to spend time with her.

Conflict tugged at him. After listening to her explanation about how she came by the ring, he had even considered that maybe she was totally innocent.

Yeh and pigs might fly too, a little voice chastised him. *Start thinking with your brain and not with your—*

He jumped as Tamsin's fingers brushed against his and she passed him the wine list. 'I'd say just go with the waiter's advice and accept the selection that's on the wine list. Unless there's something you want to choose especially. They've chosen well.' She gestured to her bag on the edge of the table. 'Would you think I was rude if I took a photo of the wine list?'

'Not at all. This is work for you.'

And it's supposed to be for me too.

He passed the wine list back to her once her phone was out of her bag.

By the time the first course had arrived, and Tam had exclaimed over the taste of each morsel that went into her mouth, Gabe had managed to steer the conversation to her past.

'So, when Mum and Dad split, I was on my own.' She lifted her eyes to meet his. 'And I have been ever since, apart from a couple of brief mistakes.' Each time he felt he was making inroads she asked him a question; she was adept at turning the tables on him. 'So, tell me about you. Where did you grow up?'

'In Melbourne. And I'm still there. Would you believe this is my first trip up here?'

'Well, you can appreciate it even more as an adult staying in a swanky apartment, rather than in the back of a Kombi van.'

'I am appreciating it, believe me.' This time the eye contact set all his nerve endings on fire, and he knew that if he was right at reading this woman, Tamsin would be spending the night at his apartment.

***

Tam tried hard not to moan in ecstasy.

They were on dessert, and the last, of the six tasting courses and her taste buds were in heaven.

Not to mention the rest of her. Somehow during the courses, Gabe had moved his chair to Tam's side of the table so—he said with a sexy smile—he could look out at the water too. Or that was the excuse he'd used, even though she wasn't protesting. The water was pitch black, and every so often a single mast light would pierce the darkness as a boat approached the marina.

Her nerve endings were tingling, and the butterflies in her stomach were moving lower each time he touched her. And he'd done that more frequently as the evening progressed.

Gabe's leg was hard up against hers as they shared the dessert from the same plate. The glasses of wine that had accompanied each course had dispelled any shyness or awkwardness and she leaned towards him as he teased her with the last spoonful of champagne jelly and Chantilly cream.

'I think this is my portion,' he said softly. Gabe was so close his breath brushed the loose tendrils of hair at the side of her face.

The spoon hovered just in front of Tam's lips and he leaned forward at the same time she did. The spoon was forgotten as their lips met and clung briefly.

She'd thought the food was heavenly, but the taste of Gabe left it for dead.

His other hand moved beneath the table and rested lightly on her thigh, and she quivered as an exquisite sensation ran through her.

'No, it's mine,' she said breathlessly. This time the moan that she held back had nothing to do with food.

'Are you ready to leave?' His eyes were coal black as they held hers. 'And more importantly will you come back to my apartment with me?'

'I am.' Her voice was breathless. 'And I will.'

'Are you happy to walk? It's only a couple of hundred metres around the bend.'

'I'll just go to the restroom and freshen up. I'll meet you in the foyer.'

Gabe moved his chair and held his hand out to help her stand.

Tam's knees trembled as he leaned forward and brushed his lips against hers. 'Don't be too long.'

Tam used the facilities and washed her hands before she sent a text to Evie.

Dinner was amazing. So is Gabe. See you both in the morning.

The reply was instant.

Be good. Be careful. Be happy.

Tam sent back a thumbs up and put her phone

away. As she looked in the mirror to tidy her hair, her eyes widened. She looked different. Leaning forward she studied herself. Her cheeks were pink and her skin glowed. But it was her eyes that told the story.

Never had she ever thought of herself as sultry before, not plain, chubby, blonde Tamsin Jones.

The woman who stared back at her had eyes that mirrored how she was feeling.

And that was what she wanted Gabe Brown to see.

Chapter Twelve

Gabe

Four hours later, Gabe stood beside the bed, staring down at the woman who had taken him to heaven and back.

Three times.

The delicate moonlight played over her face and she sighed in her sleep. How could the touch of a woman leave him feeling like this?

He turned and walked to the window, his mind full of confusion and his emotions scattered. The full moon was high in the sky and a path of moonlight walked on the water below.

Tomorrow he was going to ring Lukas Werner and ask to be taken off the job.

It wasn't fair to anybody. Even though he had been as close to Tamsin as it was possible to be, he knew he had held a little of himself back. Until he could meet with her on even ground, and be honest, he wouldn't sleep with her again.

He had a week to spend over on Pentecost Island, and even though he would give up the job, he would still try to find out the story behind the ring. Because if he didn't Lukas would put someone else on the case, and there was no way Gabe wanted that to happen.

He knew Tamsin hadn't stolen the ring. She had given herself to him tonight, and he knew there was no subterfuge in the woman in his bed.

Sucker. That little voice on his shoulder wouldn't go away now that the desire had been satisfied. He pushed it away and moved back to the bed, smiling at the scattered clothing on the bedroom floor. They hadn't even had a coffee or a drink. They had stumbled into the apartment. Lips locked together and hands feverishly exploring had sent any control he'd intended having spiralling out the window.

Quivering in his arms, Tamsin had undone the buttons on his shirt and caressed his bare chest

But it had been the murmur of her words against his lips that had tipped him over the edge. 'Take me to bed, Gabe. Please.'

He stared down at the bureau, the moonlight reflected on her jewellery. Somewhere in the frantic activity that had preceded them tumbling into bed

Tamsin had let her hair loose, and then removed the gold chain from around her neck, and placed it on the bureau with her earrings, her grandmother's ring and *the* ring.

He glanced at his phone and lifted his hand. It hovered over the phone for a few seconds as he hesitated.

Tamsin murmured in her sleep and he jumped back.

No.

Chapter Thirteen

Pippa

Thursday morning dawned fine and clear, and the weather forecast for the next few days was looking good: light south-easterly winds at five to ten knots and no rain expected, with mild temperatures day and night.

That was one problem I could tick off my list.

And boy, did I have a list.

This morning as I lay in bed worrying, Rafe tickled me in an attempt to make me chill.

'Calm down, love. We will get it *all* done. And with time to spare. You give me a list for the day, and I guarantee, I'll get it all done.'

'Thanks, babe.' I tapped my lip as I stared at the rattan fan spinning slowly above us. Despite my intention to get up early, I'd overslept, and the sun was pouring into the bedroom. 'I have to think if there's anything we've forgotten, and the girls can bring it back from Hamo.'

Rafe lay on his back beside me and ticked off

a list on his fingers.

'Food. *Check.* Tam has that under control. Drink. *Check.* Nat has already stocked the bar. He's as bad as you. He was back and forth yesterday counting bottles. Music. *Check.* Phillipe and Eliza have set up the wireless speakers, and they've tested your play list. It sounds great. Staff. *Check.* Tam is heating up the food at the house and we have the food heaters down at the bar to keep it warm, plus the two microwaves. Sienna and Evie will run it down from the house. Hostess. *Check.* You. Shuttle ferry. *Ch—*'

'Hang on.' I sat up and stared at him, with my hands over my mouth. 'Oh my God! Staff! Tam was going to interview over on Hamo. I bet she's been so busy having a good time, she's forgotten all about it. She'll have been to all the restaurants and never given it another thought. We need extras to clear the tables and wash up.' I rolled over and grabbed my phone from the bedside table and pulled Tam up on speed dial.

Her phone rang for ages and then went to her voicemail.

'What time is it?' I asked Rafe. 'She must be

out running.'

'Almost eight. Time we were up, I guess.' Rafe tugged at my hand. 'Come back and give me another cuddle. It's lonely down here.'

I leaned over and dropped a kiss on his forehead and at the same time I dialled Evie's number.

'You're no fun.' Rafe pulled a face at me and climbed out of bed, and I couldn't help admiring that sexy bare back as he walked into the ensuite.

'Keep the shower running. I'll join you as soon as I talk to Evie.' As I called after him, Evie picked up.

'Thank God,' I said. 'Is Tamsin there? She's not answering.'

'Ah, no. She's not.'

'Damn. Do you know if she's talked to those casual staff she was talking about getting for the opening? I thought she would have texted me by now.'

'Sorry, she hasn't mentioned it, but no, I don't think she has.'

'Where is she now? How long will she be?'

Silence.

'Evie, what's going on. This is important.'

'Ah, she's met someone. A guy.'

'Great timing.' I rolled my eyes. 'Before you come back across this afternoon, can you *please* make sure she rings me.'

'Will do. See you later, Pippa.'

I threw the phone away and tried to control my temper. Why had Tamsin done this to me?

I stormed into the bathroom, and even the sight of Rafe in the shower didn't improve my mood.

'Bloody Tamsin,' I almost screeched so he could hear me over the running water.

'What's wrong now?'

'She's found herself a man. Bloody dreadful timing.'

The shower door opened and before I had time to move, Rafe's arm shot out and I was in the shower with him.

'Rafe! I've still got my PJs on.'

'I can remedy that.' His grin was wicked as he proceeded to show me how.

An hour later, my mood had improved considerably—thanks to my gorgeous man—and we were down at the bar.

'Are you calm now?' Rafe spread his arms. 'See. Now what can you see that still needs doing?''

I looked around and smiled. 'Um, nothing.'

Nat stood up from where he had been crouched behind the bar counter. 'Don't panic, Pippa. Everything is under control. Except for poor Nell. She's on the phone to Jiminy trying to organise a fleet. She's closed off the bookings for tomorrow night.'

'Really? We've reached two hundred?'

'Um.' Nat stood there and scratched his head as he flicked a glance at Rafe. 'I think it's gone over three hundred acceptances. Plus the unknowns are the sailors who'll just pull into the bay. And the ABC just rang from Mackay. They're sending a camera crew. Nell was looking for you half an hour ago. You have to call them back.'

'Holy hell!' I jumped at Rafe and threw my arms around him. 'We're going to be on TV! Oh my God, I *knew* I forgot something. I haven't got anything to wear to the opening.'

'Really? This is the woman who took a whole day to move her clothes up to the house?' He raised his eyebrows and hugged me back. 'Give Tam another call and get her to bring you something back. She knows you well enough.'

I pulled my phone out and hurried to the beach where the reception was better. This time Tam picked up straight away.

'Tam, where the hell are you? I need you.' I was almost crying; it was a mix of jubilation and worry.

'What's wrong? And I'm still in bed. I'm on a break remember?' Even though her words were sassy, she sounded much more relaxed.

'Have you got a pen? I need you to make a list. What time will you be back?' Before she could answer, I reeled it off. 'We'll need more disposable plates and napkins, about a hundred disposable wine glasses, and we need those staff you were going to get to come over and maybe two more and I need a new outfit. Can you do all that and be back soon?'

Tam giggled.

She giggled at me!

'Tam? Are you there?'

Another giggle and the penny dropped when I heard a deeper voice in the background.

'Tamsin Jones, are you listening to me?'

'I am. Text me what you want, Pip. We'll be back about four.'

'I will, but this might hurry you up, Tam. We have three hundred plus coming to the bar opening. *Tomorrow! Three hundred!*'

Her screech was extremely satisfying. 'Oh my God, we won't have enough food. Gabe, I have to go. Pip, send me that list. I'll go shopping now. Oh hell, Gabe, I can't wear this dress shopping. How will I get back to the hotel? *Text me, Pippa!*'

The call disconnected and I sent a text, feeling much better that Tam was now back on the ball. I knew I shouldn't have agreed to them leaving the island so close to the opening.

Chapter Fourteen

Tamsin

Gabe was an absolute saviour; he somehow found a buggy while Tam was in his shower. As soon as she was out and dried, she pulled her new dress on, ran her fingers through her wet hair and left it loose, scooped her jewellery into the new bag, and raced out carrying her blue shoes.

Gabe grinned as Tam ran out. 'Your chariot awaits, madame.'

She drew in a breath and reached up and kissed his cheek. 'Oh, I so owe you big time. I'm sorry to race off, but I have to get back to the island.'

Tam laughed aloud as Gabe roared down the hill as fast as he could in the electric buggy. She kept glancing across at him; his dark hair was blowing in the breeze, and he looked a lot more casual than he had when she had first met him.

Had that only been last night? And what a night! Tam felt as though she'd known him for ages.

Five minutes later Gabe pulled the buggy up outside the hotel foyer.

'Do you want to come up,' Tam asked.

He shook his head. 'No, I'll leave you to it, but will you have time to see me before you leave?'

'Of course. I'll make time.' She leaned over and kissed him and his arms went around her. For a brief wild moment, Tam forgot all about the bar opening and Pippa's instructions. She pulled away reluctantly when someone called her name. Evie was standing beside the buggy.

'I see Pippa got on to you.'

'Yes. Can you be ready to leave about noon?'

Evie nodded and held her hand out for the bag and shoes. 'I can.'

Tam turned back to Gabe. 'Can you meet me at the marina around eleven thirty? I should be finished by then. I'm sorry I have to rush, but I hope you'll come over to the opening.'

'As long as I can get to the island, I'll be there. I promise.'

'I'll call Jiminy and make sure he gets you there.'

'Great. I'll see you in a couple of hours.'

Tam hurried inside with Evie close behind

her. 'Where's Sienna?'

'She's getting packed up, and then we were going to grab a quick breakfast. Have you eaten yet?'

Tam shook her head and yawned as they went into the elevator. 'I haven't even had a coffee.'

'Have you had any sleep?'

Tam simply smiled.

'Seriously, did you have a good night? The dinner, I mean. I don't expect you to kiss and tell,' Evie's smile was wicked. 'But judging by your satisfied glow, not to mention the see-you-soon kiss, the rest goes without saying.'

Tam folded her arms and smiled again. 'Mmm, dinner was incredible.'

'And Gabe?'

'He's great, and he's coming to the opening.'

'I heard.'

'So, what about you and Sienna? Did you have a good night?'

'We did. We ended up in the bar downstairs and met some nice people. They're coming to the opening too.'

'Oh, that's great,' Tam said. 'I don't feel so

bad for going out.'

The elevator door pinged open and Tam marshalled her thoughts. 'If I give you a shopping list, could you and Sienna get a few things for me while I chase up the staff I need to hire?'

##

An hour later, the girls had had a quick breakfast at the hotel, packed up and checked out. Sienna wanted to know all about the meal, and Tam guessed she was digging for more information, but she hugged that part of the night to herself. All she would say was, 'I had the best time.'

As they ate, Tam made a list and smiled as she added frozen scallops to the list along with a dozen boxes of assorted frozen foods, puff pastry and cheese and fresh herbs. If Pippa was accurate with the numbers, they would need every bit of it, and she'd make up more fresh pastries when she got back.

The girls loaded their cases into a buggy and headed off to the marina to drop them onto Evie's yacht before they went shopping. Tam headed to a small bar where she knew some of the casual staff. She had instant success there, booked four casual staff to come over to Pentecost Island tomorrow, and then went in search of an outfit for Pippa.

Tam was going to pay for it herself and give it to Pippa as a gift to make up for being such a cow over the past week.

She was finished by eleven, and she smiled as she hurried back to the marina, carrying the parcels. The warm glow from last night still hadn't left her. She really hoped that Gabe's research would mean that there was a likelihood of work on Hamo. Tam made a mental note to ask Nat if he could have a word to Gabe. And she had to ring Jiminy now to make sure he got a ride over tomorrow.

She would be extremely happy if Gabe stayed around for a while.

***

Gabe

Gabe opened his laptop to pull up the files on Tamsin and consider how much, if any, information he would give Lukas. Never had he become so emotionally involved with a woman in such a short time, and he knew it was impossible to stay on the case. It was not ethical, and if he had to choose it would be Tamsin.

Once he looked at the notes he'd made, he'd decide what he was going to say to Lukas.

His dilemma was that he knew Tamsin was innocent. But it was also unethical not to tell Lukas that she was in possession of the ring.

Or a ring that was very similar—okay identical—to the one he'd seen a photograph of in Melbourne.

And how do you know she's innocent? Logic chimed in. *Because you took her to dinner and then she came back to your bed?*

No, Gabe thought. His instincts told him that Tamsin hadn't stolen anything. When he'd asked her about the ring, there had been no hesitation and no guile. She'd said it was a gift and he believed her.

You're a fool.

If she'd stolen it, why would she wear it to dinner, and flaunt it? He rationalised to himself, if she'd taken it for the money, she would have sold it.

He stared at the screen on his laptop. He'd been so keen to get out to meet her last night, he'd not done any more digging. Would it be better to ask her straight out about the ring and tell her why he was here?

Chapter Fifteen

Tamsin

Sienna and Evie had done well with the shopping and the small fridge on Evie's boat was filled with boxes of frozen spring rolls, curry puffs and samosas.

'There's a couple of polystyrene boxes in the hold, too. With the other stuff you wanted,' Evie said. 'I knew there wouldn't be enough space in the galley.'

'Thanks, girls. That was a great help.' Tam looked at her watch and frowned. It was heading for noon, and there was no sign of Gabe yet. She was keen to get back to the island, because she was going to spend all afternoon and night in the kitchen. She would only use the bought food if they ran out.

'Ready to head out now?' Evie asked.

'I asked Gabe to come down, just give him another ten. He must have been held up.'

'No prob. I'll go and grab a takeaway coffee. Want one?'

'Yes, please. Double shot skinny latte.'

Evie and Sienna headed along the wharf to the marina coffee shop, and Tam smiled as she spotted Gabe heading along the concourse. When he looked down at the water, she waved, and he waved back. A little tremor shivered down her legs as she waited for him to walk down.

God, she had it bad. That's what she got for being on the island for so long with no socialising. The first guy who came along . . .

As Gabe approached, Tam stepped off the boat and waited on the wharf, and that shaky feeling came back.

'Thanks for coming to see us off,' she said. 'The girls have just gone to get a coffee before we leave.'

Tam was surprised when Gabe didn't touch her; he seemed preoccupied.

'I've talked to Jiminy, and he's got you a place on the first boat over tomorrow afternoon. If that suits, of course. If you still want to come.' Her voice was hesitant. 'Don't feel as though you have to.'

'Of course, I'll be there.' Finally, she got a

brief smile.

'Everything okay?' She was immediately cross with herself for asking. That's how the relationship with Chad had panned out. She'd always needed reassurance.

'Yeah, fine. Sorry I've been working and I'm still in that head space.'

She looked up when she felt his touch. Gabe's arms went around her, and he dropped a kiss on her lips.

'It's going to be lonely here tonight,' he said softly. 'I'll miss you.'

'I'd love to stay but work calls. But I'll see you tomorrow night. I'm going to be busy, but I'll make sure that I spend some time with you after the rush is gone. I'll introduce you to Rafe, he'll be good company for you while we're all rushing about. Actually, if you'd like to stay the night, I could find you a bed.'

His gaze was intense. 'Would you be in it?'

'Depends if you wanted me there.'

'Oh, yes, Tamsin Jones, that is a given.' His tone was harsh, and Tam pulled back in surprise. It sounded as though he didn't want it to be that way.

'Are you sure you're okay? I hope I haven't upset you by taking off so quickly. I really have to go back, it's nothing to do with you.'

'I know that. And I'll see you tomorrow afternoon. Can I call in and see you if you're working?'

'I'd be cross if you didn't. When you come out to the island, you'll see the house.' She laughed. 'Not the one at the top of the hill, the old 1930s house at the northern end of the beach. I'm sure to be in the kitchen.' She stood on her toes and this time she kissed him. 'Here come the girls now. I'll look forward to tomorrow.'

Gabe pulled out his phone. 'I don't have your number. What's yours and I'll text you, so you have mine. If you feel like a chat later tonight, give me a call.'

Her phone pinged and she smiled. If he was exchanging phone numbers, he didn't intend disappearing. She'd worried for a moment when he'd been late and then seemed distant.

As they motored out to the channel Tam stood

on the back deck and watched Gabe as he walked along the wharf and through the marina until he disappeared. His strange mood had taken a bit of her glow away.

With a shrug she turned and walked up to the front of the boat. She'd had fun for the past two days and now it was time to go back to work.

Maybe she should have left it at that, and not invited Gabe over.

##

When they arrived back, Pentecost Island was a flurry of activity. The moorings at the front of the bay were all taken, and Evie commented on the number of boats in Back Bay as they'd approached the island. Pippa had obviously been watching out for them; she and Rafe were waiting on the wharf as they motored into the bay.

'Welcome back, ladies. Did you have a fabulous time?' Rafe took the rope that Evie threw across the deck and secured them to the first bollard. Tam went down to the galley and got as many boxes as she could carry in one trip up the narrow stairs and took them up to the deck.

'Did you get everything you needed?' Pippa asked.

'Everything and more,' Tam said. 'More food than we'll ever need, glasses, plates, four staff and a fabulous outfit for you to wear.'

'Good to see you back and happy. I hear you had a good time.' Pippa grinned at her.

'God, is nothing private around here?' Tam complained, but her grin stayed in place.

'So, who is he?' Pippa wasn't going to give up.

Tam wagged her finger. 'Be patient. You'll meet Gabe tomorrow. He's coming over with Jiminy.'

'I'm really pleased you took the break, Tam.' Pippa stepped over the side of the boat and gave her a brief hug. 'And I'm sorry I was short-tempered with you. Now, what else needs carrying up?'

Tam pointed to the cartons that held the plastic glasses and disposable plates. 'You take those, and I'll go down and get your bag from the boutique. You are going to love what I bought. As soon as I walked in it, I saw it and it screamed Pippa at me.'

'Ooh, I can't wait. Thanks, sweets.'

Tam headed straight up to the kitchen and turned the two large ovens on, before taking her bag to her room.

'Welcome back. I hear you enjoyed yourself.' Nell stood in the doorway, a pencil tucked behind her ear, and her glasses on top of her head. 'And you look great.'

'Must be the new hair colour,' Tam said.

'And the happy face. I'm pleased you had fun. We missed you, but we almost starved. Nat and I weren't game to eat anything out of the cool room.' Nell chuckled. 'We had baked beans on toast because we figured you wouldn't need them for the bar opening!'

'What, both nights? Baked beans aren't very romantic.'

'No, we had a barbeque up at Rafe and Pippa's last night.'

'I'm pleased to hear you didn't starve.'

'Don't forget we have sunset drinks this afternoon.'

'I doubt if I'll have time,' Tam said.

'Make time,' Pippa appeared in the doorway behind Nell. 'We've got something to tell you.'

'We?' Tam asked.

'Eliza and I. Well, mainly Eliza, but it is something that is going to make you both very happy. Well, I hope it is. I'm so excited, I've barely slept.'

'Spill, Pippa. You know I hate surprises. But be quick.' Tam picked up her bag. 'I have to get to work.'

'Nope, you have to wait. I'll see you down on the beach at six. If you need a hand in the kitchen, call me. I'll be down in the bar. We're putting the fairy lights up.' Pippa laughed. 'Evie's already on the mower.'

'We've all got a stack to do.'

'See you both later.' Pippa went out to the veranda and Tam was pleased to hear her singing as she crossed the lawn. It had been a long time since she'd heard that.

'I can give you a hand to wash dishes and stuff, if you like,' Nell said. 'I'm going to turn the phone off and put it onto the voice message. The huts are booked out for the first month now. I'll deal with any messages they leave. Once we get on Trip Advisor and review sites, I think we are going to take off.'

'Not just curiosity?' Tam walked toward the door. 'You don't think it will fade?'

'A bit of that,' Nell said, 'but still lots of enquiries about forward bookings. I've been on the phone so much, I've got little else done. Nat's got the bar organised today while I've been on the phone. At this rate, we're going to need a couple of receptionists before the guests arrive.'

Tam paused in the doorway. 'Oh, that reminds me, I told Gabe I'd book him in for tomorrow night. I've already organised for Jiminy to bring him over. He was going to see about a hut too. Can you just add him to the numbers for tomorrow please?'

'Gabe, hey?' Nell smiled. 'Unusual name and the second time I've heard it this week. We had a Gabe Brown book in for the opening, and a hut late next week.'

Tam smiled at Gabe's enthusiasm to come over. 'He's rung already? He must be keen. I said I'd sort it for him.'

Nell frowned. 'No, that booking was made a couple of days ago. Before you went away, I think.'

Tam frowned. 'Are you sure that was the name?'

'I think so. Do you want me to check?'

'Thanks. I'll just put my bag away and get changed.'

Nell had to be wrong; either that or there were two Gabe Browns. She tried to think back to their conversation about the island. She'd mentioned the bar opening to Gabe the first night that they'd met at the yacht club, and she was sure she'd offered to book him in, and he'd said he'd let her know. And then after they'd got together, he'd said he would come.

Either Nell had the wrong name or there were two Gabe Browns coming tomorrow night. Nell was a while and Tam was already chopping herbs when she came back.

'Definitely Gabe Brown,' she said. 'He booked on Tuesday morning. One person for the opening, and then he's booked one of the huts from Tuesday week for three days.'

'There has to be another Gabe Brown, because

he didn't mention it at all.'

'Have you got his mobile number?'

'I have. But I'll have to look it up.' Tam went over to the window. Her phone was on the windowsill. She picked it up, opened her messages and read out his number.

'Yep. One and the same.' Nell nodded. 'You must have been destined to meet over there. How romantic.'

'Isn't it just? Destiny,' Tam said, but she didn't say what she was thinking. She wasn't sure what was going on. But if there was one thing she hated; it was a man who was not honest. Why hadn't Gabe told her he was already booked in?

Maybe he was trying to stroke her ego, so she'd think she was the attraction.

Tam chopped the herbs with so much force, she almost sliced her finger off.

Calm down and stop stressing over something so trivial, she told herself.

But the experience with Chad had left her fragile.

Trust didn't come easy to Tam, and she would

never condone dishonesty.

Chapter Sixteen

Tamsin

The afternoon flew, but by the time Nell poked her head around the door at five thirty, Tam was almost done. She'd thawed and filled three batches of bought filo pastry with feta cheese and basil stuffing, made six dozen mini-quiches and had two bowls of spare filling in the cool room. Hopefully, the backup frozen food wouldn't be needed. The scallops were thawing in the cool room, ready to be sizzled in the sauce she'd made. If they were needed.

'Almost done?' Nell asked.

'All done. I'm just going to have a quick wash and get changed. Do you want to walk down together? I'd like to check out the bar.'

'Sure. Nat's still down there with Rafe. They've been stringing fairy lights all day.'

Tam threw her apron into the laundry and had a quick wash before she changed into one of her dresses. Nell was sitting in a hammock on the veranda. She jumped up when Tam walked out and they headed across the lawn together

'It looks a bit different to the day we arrived, doesn't it,' Nell said.

'Everything's different since then. It's hard to believe how much has changed in the six months we've been here.'

Tam linked her arm through Nell's. 'Rafe and Pippa, you and Nat, Eliza and Phillipe, and now Sienna's arrived too.'

'And you and this Gabe guy?'

'Early days, yet, Nellie. And you know me. I don't give my heart easily.'

'Neither do I, and look at me. Who knows what's around the corner?'

'Speaking of which, do you have any idea what this is all about down at the beach?'

'No idea, but Pippa's been jumping around for a couple of days. She's been like the Eveready Battery bunny.'

'And Eliza?'

'I haven't seen much of her. She and Phillipe were out on his boat this morning, but they really pulled their weight yesterday. Helped move all the tables and carried bottles from the shed to the bar.'

Pippa was waiting for them at the bar and looked pleased when Tam widened her eyes as she looked around. 'Wow, this looks great.'

Each table had a candle in the middle next to a small jar filled with flowers. The fairy lights that the guys had been putting up twinkled on the exterior of the building and along the top of the bar inside. Four long trestle tables filled the opening that led out to the rainforest.

'I thought we could put some of the food along there, as well as the girls walking around with trays of food, and there'll be somewhere for guests to put their empty plates and glasses. But if you'd prefer another arrangement that works better for you, just say.' Pippa bit her lip. 'There's not going to be enough seating for most of the guests, but I never in my dreams thought we'd get so many here.'

'I'm sure they'll wander down to the beach and sit on the sand,' Tam said.

'Yes, Phillipe and Nat and Rafe hauled some fallen logs out of the forest yesterday and they've made some seats down below the huts.'

'I hope they checked for snakes and spiders.' Tam shivered.

'Yes, I made them, and then I sprayed them with insect spray too.' Pippa put a hand to her head. 'You know, I think I just want this all to be over. Life can go back to normal.'

'You really think so? I've got bad news for you, girlfriend. This is the new normal.' Tam winked at Nell. 'Whose idea was it to start a resort anyway?'

Tam and Nell stood on either side of Pippa and they linked arms. 'You'll love every minute of it. We all will,' Nell said.

'Did you try your dress on?' Tam asked.

'Yes, it's perfect, thank you. Remind me to pay you for it.'

'No, it's a gift to celebrate the opening, and an apology for my crappy behaviour.'

'Thank you. Do you girls know how much I love you? And how much I appreciate that we're in this together? More than you know,' Tam heard Pippa add quietly at the end.

'Goes without saying, Pip,' Tam said.

They stepped onto the beach. Eliza and Sienna

were over near the rocks, and Tam laughed.

'Gone are the days of the old picnic rug.'

A table was set near the water with a tablecloth and a tray of crystal glasses. Two candles flickered in the slight breeze. The sun hovered above the mountains and the fading light bathed the distant mainland in a purple duskiness. The last rays of the sun reflected on a bank of cloud hovering above the peaks shining in a coral flame.

The sea was still and the lights of the dozen or so boats in their bay winked in the growing darkness. A lone star gradually appeared in the clear sky above.

'It's breathtaking, isn't it?' Pippa whispered. 'At times like this, I know Auntie Vi is up there looking down on us, and saying go for it, girls.'

'I'm sure she knows, Pip.' Tam crossed to the table and raised her eyebrows. 'Moet?'

'Two bottles,' Nell said.

'It's a very special night,' Pippa answered softly, and her voice shook.

Tam was surprised to see the gleam of tears in Pippa's eyes. 'What's going on. Pip?'

'You'll see. Come on.'

Eliza handed them each a glass of champagne. Tam thought she looked nervous.

'Thanks, Eliza. Hi, Sienna.'

'Hey, Tam. Good to see you,' Eliza said. 'We haven't had time to catch up much since we got back.'

'We've all been busy.' Tam chuckled. 'We were busy over on Hamo, I guess. So, what's this news? Is this an early celebration?'

Eliza glanced over at Pippa before she spoke.

'I don't know where to start. Would you believe I'm nervous?'

'There's no need to be,' Pippa said.

Eliza took a deep breath and Tam waited. She glanced over at Nell; her eyes were fixed on Eliza. Sienna was smiling and Tam figured whatever this news was, Sienna already knew.

'To cut a long story short,' Eliza said quickly, 'like Pippa, I received an inheritance. It was unexpected, and one I didn't want.' Her lip trembled as she stared at Tam. 'Tam, you saved my life when I came to the island, and I will be forever in your debt. Then you all looked after me and sheltered me in a very difficult time. I'm investing in the island, and I want you and Nell to be a part of that.'

Pippa interrupted. 'With Eliza's contribution, we're building fifteen more huts; the plans are already in for a separate restaurant with a commercial kitchen and we're doing another building to house the day spa that Sienna will be looking after.'

Tam's mouth dropped open. 'It must have been a damn good inheritance.' Nell looked shell-shocked and Sienna was smiling. She reached over and squeezed Tam's hand

Eliza nodded. 'It was. I'm matching the valuation of the island dollar for dollar. And that's not all.'

Pippa lifted the champagne bottle and topped up our glasses. 'Nell and Tam, you have been a part of my life for a long time, and I—we—want you to be a part of this.'

'But we already are,' Tam said.

'I know, but it's going to be formalised.'

'How?' Nell and Tam both asked at the same time.

'It's a gift from Eliza,' Pippa said. 'To each of

you, so you can be a true part of the company.'

Eliza glanced at Pippa again, and Pippa continued. 'Today when I put your monthly salary into your accounts, a second deposit went in too. What we would like you to do is invest that money back into the resort. That way you both become shareholders and will share in the profits over the years.' Pippa's hand was shaking with emotion as she lifted her glass and took a sip. 'But it's entirely up to you. There's no pressure. If you don't want to, and you just want to keep the money as savings, that's all good. It's yours to keep, from Eliza. Nothing changes, whether you accept or not. You might like to talk to your accountant or solicitor about the way you want to do it. That's if you want to join into the company we've set up.'

Tam shook her head and looked at Nell. Her cheeks were pink, and her eyes were round.

'I don't know what to say,' Nell said. 'Apart from, yes, I'd love to be a part of whatever you've set up.'

'Tam?' Pippa looked at her. 'Any thoughts?'

Tam shook her head slowly from side to side,

before she put her glass on the table and walked over to Eliza. She opened her arms and hugged her. 'You didn't have to do that. You don't owe me. I'm still processing this.' Tam stepped back and looked at Pippa and Eliza. 'How much exactly are we talking about? That's gone into our accounts, I mean?' She glanced at Nell. 'I think we need a lot more information before we can we agree to anything.'

Chapter Seventeen

Gabe

One thing Gabe had avoided was logging into Tamsin's bank account. His ethical standards would not let him do that unless a case got to the stage where it was unavoidable. He'd already done a background check, and an assets check using databases that were available without even going to the dark web. If the average person knew how much of their information was held on public record databases, they would be very uncomfortable.

Privacy? That didn't exist in the days of databases. A competent investigator could retrieve a wealth of information and when searched by someone who knew what they were doing, they could build a detailed profile about a person's wealth and circumstances. And none of it was illegal.

But hacking into a private bank account was.

He could log in to Tamsin's account, make sure there was nothing untoward there, and then ring Lukas and tell him she was—

And tell him she was what?

Gabe rubbed his hand over his face. Tell him that yes, Tamsin Jones was in possession of a ring that fitted the description of the missing piece, but she was not a thief.

And why do you think that, Gabe?

Because I just know.

Even after knowing her less than twenty-four hours?

Yes, I am sure.

If Lukas objected to closing the case, Gabe knew he had to come up with a very good reason for being sure that Tamsin was innocent.

Maybe.

Damn, he'd never been so bloody confused in his life. How could one woman make all logic fly out the window?

Think with your brain, man.

Gabe shook his head; it wasn't just because they'd spent the night together

Yeah, okay, that had been incredible.

But it was Tamsin, the woman, who fascinated him.

If this relationship was going to work, he was

going to be upfront and tell Tamsin why he had contrived their meeting. And ask her outright about the ring.

But not until the bar opening was over; he didn't want to upset her.

And he *would* like to spend more time getting to know her. Problem was he had to find a job up this way. There was nothing to keep him in Melbourne.

Seriously, you've known her how long?

But I know.

That was enough, he would look at the bank account, then get the hell out of her private business. After that he'd ring Lukas and tell him he was off the case.

Gabe glanced down at the screen as the bank app logged in.

And stared.

At the huge deposit that had gone into Tamsin's account overnight.

He shook his head and looked again. He shut the lid of his laptop.

You're a fool man. You've been duped big time.

It took him ten minutes to open the laptop and log in again. Then Gabe stared at that bank statement page for a long time as his thoughts whirred around. He closed the browser and sat there and wondered what the hell he had done.

Or more to the point, what the hell Tamsin Jones had done. She'd sold the ring.

He put his phone away; there was no point calling Lukas Werner now. He'd committed to this case, and now he was more determined than ever to find out the truth.

Maybe that was her whole reason for going to Hamilton Island. She'd been damn keen to get away from him after coffee yesterday and then again this morning.

Chapter Eighteen

Pippa

Our opening day dawned bright and clear, and the mood on the island was upbeat. Because everyone had worked so hard, there was little to do apart from the finishing touches.

We'd set the starting time for five o'clock, with the short official opening by the Whitsundays mayor at six-thirty. Cold finger food on the tables until then, and then Tam would serve the hot food when the official stuff was over.

I couldn't keep still. I dropped my coffee mug on the kitchen tiles as soon as the day began, and then I searched high and low for my hairdryer before Rafe pointed to it in the vanity drawer where it always lived.

He stood behind me as I dried strands of my apricot-coloured hair one by one. I usually didn't bother, but I wanted it to look perfect for tonight.

'Aren't you doing this a bit early,' he said as he lifted a handful of already dry hair and nuzzled my neck.

'Probably. But I can do it again this afternoon, if it needs it.'

My hand shook, and I dropped the dryer on the floor. Rafe ignored it and his hands slid down my shoulders and caressed my bare back.

'I think you need something to fill in the morning and take your mind off tonight.'

I turned in his arms. 'And what are you suggesting?' My voice was low and husky.

'I think we should go back to bed. You probably need some rest so you're bright and energetic tonight.'

'Do you?' I murmured against his mouth. 'And guess what, I'm feeling pretty energetic right now.'

##

We did end up dozing after I had expended quite a lot of my pent-up energy, and when I woke, I was nestled in Rafe's arms.

I extricated myself and sat up quickly. 'Crumbs, what time is it?'

'It's just gone ten,' he said lazily.

'It's time to get up. We need to get organised.'

'We are organised.'

'No. It's opening day. The girls will think I'm being slack. I should be down there.'

'I'm sure they won't. Now, my darling, can I take your attention away from the opening for a few minutes or will it make you cross?' He pulled me back down next to him.

I gave him a mock frown. 'Are you saying you didn't have my undivided attention before?'

His grin still gave me butterflies in my stomach. 'Now you *are* cross.'

'You never upset me, Rafe. What do you want to talk about? Your next book?'

He laughed. 'Nothing as mundane as that.'

'Is something wrong?' A flurry of worry surfaced for a moment and then I knew I was being silly.

'No, everything is perfect. Are you happy?'

'I've never been happier.'

'Truly?' Rafe propped himself up on one elbow and looked down at me.

'Truly. Let me tell you why. One, you love me. Two, Tam and Nell were very receptive to

Eliza's proposal last night. Three, our resort is opening tonight. Four—'

He silenced me with his lips on mine. 'Have I told you how much I love you today?'

'No.' I put my arms around his neck and kept his head close as he went to move back.

'I love you to the moon and back, Pippa Carmichael. And speaking of getting organised, there *is* one thing we do need to decide on.'

'Oh no, what have I forgotten?' I panicked. 'I knew something would go wrong today.'

'It's only going to get busier here, now that you're about to open.'

'It is. So?'

'I think we need to decide on a date for our wedding. What do you think? Do we really have any reason to wait?'

Love for this man blossomed through me. I held Rafe's eyes and shook my head. 'No reason to wait whatsoever.'

'You choose,' he said, as he reached up and stroked my cheek.

'No, you choose,' I said lacing my hands

around the back of his neck.

'Really, you'll trust me to pick a date?'

'You pick the date and I'll agree.'

'The first of November.'

I tipped my head to the side and worked out I would have six weeks to get organised.

'Done. Now kiss me and then we need to get to work.'

I really loved the way Rafe always did as I asked.

***

Tamsin

Tam was remarkably organised.

And calm.

So calm, that mid-morning she went looking for something to do. After their drinks on the beach last night, she'd worked until midnight figuring she might as well work late, get it all done and then clean up the one mess.

Everything that needed to be thawed today was now out on the sink and the countertops, the kitchen was spotless, and she'd lined up all the serving platters and tongs she'd need tonight on the table. She'd pressed her black and white checked pants and white cotton shirt and even ran the iron over the bandana that held her hair back while she worked.

The casual wait staff were arriving at noon, so they would be able to take the food down to the fridges in the bar during the afternoon.

Although she was focused on the food preparation, and the amount that they would need, her mind was still whirling with Eliza's proposal. When she had told them last night that one hundred thousand dollars had been deposited in each of their bank accounts, Tam had felt faint.

If she could find Nell, she'd see what she was thinking. Last night, they'd just looked at each other, almost disbelieving. Tam had already decided that she would put her share back into the resort. She felt good about it and would feel as though she was a true part of Ma Carmichael's.

She was still blown away by what Eliza had done and felt a bit guilty that she had been so peeved with her before they'd gone over to Hamilton Island.

Tam wandered along the veranda and stuck her head in the office, but there was no sign of Nell. The message light was blinking on both phones, but she ignored them knowing Nell would have it under control.

Stepping off the veranda, she looked around but there was no sign of Nell or Evie. The only sound was the wind in the trees above. The day was calm and peaceful; as though the island was holding its breath waiting for the madness to descend later.

With a shrug, Tam headed for the bar.

Eliza and Phillipe were sitting at an outside table soaking up the sun. Phillipe was a quiet man; always content to sit back and let the conversation go around him. As she approached, he leaned over and kissed Eliza's neck. He moved back, and the look in his eyes left Tam in no doubt how he felt about Eliza.

She sighed. It was the same way that Gabe had looked at her from the moment they'd met. That trembly feeling ran down her legs.

'Hey, you pair. What's happening?' she called out as she walked over.

'Hi, Tam. Come and sit with us.' Eliza

gestured towards one of the spare seats. 'We were thinking about having a wine. We'll be too busy tonight. I'll grab a bottle and some glasses.'

'It's early.'

'It's a special day, and I know in a little while, we'll be in a mad flurry.'

'We will, and I think it will be a late one. Pippa's talking about a party for the staff after the bar closes too,' Tam said.

'Sounds good.' Eliza stood, and Nat and Nell walked up from the beach.

'Come and join the early party,' Tam called out.

'What party?' Nell asked as they came over.

'The party before chaos hits.'

'I'll never say no to a party.' Nell yawned and Nat looped his arm around her shoulder.

'The phones are blinking up in the office, Nell,' Tam said. 'I didn't want to touch them.'

'I know. I put a message on saying the office was closed for the opening and we were full.'

'Wise move. It does feels strange though.' Tam shook her head with a chuckle. 'Despite our two days away we're really organised.'

'It's the quiet before a storm. Just wait for it.'

A noisy motor broke the calm as a dinghy headed towards the beach. Nat pointed to the boats that were moored offshore. 'That's why we were down there. We had two lots come in their dinghies to see if they could come to the bar yet. I'll go and sort this lot out.'

Tam counted the boats. 'Fifteen. More have come in this morning. It's like an invasion.'

'Think of the business.' Pippa's voice came from behind them.

As Tam turned, Evie walked through the bar with Sienna. 'Great timing. We're all here.'

'A good chance to have a meeting, and make sure we all know what we're doing tonight.'

Tam sat back and smiled as Pippa stood and counted off the things to be done and made sure they each knew their allocated tasks. Pippa was wearing one of her culotte suits and she'd wound her hair into a French braid. Her cheeks were pink, and she looked really happy, and the way she looked over to Rafe with a loving expression as she spoke made Tam happy.

'Okay, so everyone knows what they have to do, and when?' Pippa asked.

Everyone nodded and Evie and Nell got up to head back to their jobs.

'Wait,' Pippa said. 'One more thing.' She held out her hand to Rafe and he walked over and put his arm around her shoulder. 'Today's going to be a great practice run, because we've got another function coming up in six weeks.'

'Six weeks?' Tam echoed. Surely the restaurant wouldn't be open by then?

'What sort of function?' Eliza asked.

Pippa's smile was sweet, and Tam thought how beautiful she looked today.

'A wedding. We thought we might have a practice run and offer the island for weddings.'

'What do you mean by a practice run?' Tam asked.

'Rafe and I are getting married on the first of November.'

Chapter Nineteen

Tam

Tam crouched in front of the oven and rearranged the trays. Cherry and Amanda, the two girls who were working in the kitchen with her, had left to take the first trays of cold finger foods to the bar. Tessa and Mirabelle were helping Nat and Phillipe behind the bar. Wine and beer were complimentary for the first half hour and Pippa's advertising ploy had obviously worked. No wonder they were expecting over three hundred guests.

Tam closed her eyes, hoping that she had enough food, that it would stay hot, and that it would be well received. If the food wasn't up to scratch, the word would get around very quickly.

Maybe she shouldn't have taken the two days off. Maybe that had been selfish. But then she wouldn't have met Gabe.

Although her focus was totally on the food and the next two hours, excited anticipation about seeing Gabe soon rippled through her. They hadn't talked since they'd exchanged numbers.

Tam turned the oven temperature down a little; it was almost time to go to the bar. Pippa wanted them all there for the speeches.

The countertop was lined with trays ready to go into the ovens and the microwaves and Tam had written down the order the food was to be heated when the current load was heated through and taped the instructions to the table.

Cherry rushed back and picked up another two trays of the nibbles that Tam had waiting. 'My God, its buzzing down there. There are so many people arriving. I stopped counting the tenders on the beach when I got to fifty. And most of the guests are in fancy dress. Oh, and before I forget there's a guy waiting out on the steps. He wants to talk to you. A tall guy with dark—' Cherry's voice trailed off as Tam ran out of the kitchen, almost bumping into Amanda at the door.

'Sorry. The list's on the table. I'll be back as soon as the speeches are done.' Tam hurried onto the veranda and stopped, pushing back the stray curls that had fallen from the bandanna. She smoothed her hands down her white shirt, took a deep breath and walked along to the steps.

'Hello,' she said shyly. 'Long time no see.'

Gabe was standing on the top step. His black Hawaiian shirt was patterned with hot pink flowers and his boardshorts were white.

'You got here okay,' she added.

'Yes, I did. I came over on Jiminy's first trip. I've been down in the bar.'

'Did you meet anyone? Pippa or Rafe? Did you see Evie and Sienna?'

He shook his head. 'No, I didn't want to intrude. Everyone was busy, although I did say hello to Evie very briefly. She was carrying around trays of wine.' He took one step towards her and then stopped. 'I won't hold you up. I just wanted to let you know that I came over.'

'I'm very pleased and it's okay. I'm just going down now. Everything's under control in the kitchen, and Pip wants us all there for the official bit. Will you walk down with me?'

Gabe nodded, but didn't offer his arm or take her hand or anything.

Tam chatted as they walked down. 'Once the

hot food goes out about seven, I'll be busy for an hour and a half and then I'll be free for the night.'

'That's good.'

'Yes, I'll come back up and get changed. I didn't even think about fancy dress. I've got a tropical print dress, that will have to do.' She knew she was babbling, but Gabe seemed disinclined to talk. There was no way she was going to ask him if everything was okay; if he had a problem, she would be disappointed, but she was not going to beg for his attention.

'Did you get a chance to follow up what you wanted to find out about?'

Gabe stared. 'What did I want to follow up?'

'The possibility of IT work. I'll introduce you to Nat later.'

'Oh, sorry, yes. I did, and thanks, that would be good.'

As they walked down the path, the noise from the bar got louder. Music, laughter and voices filled the air and rose to a crescendo the closer they got.

'This feels so funny. It's usually quiet here.'

Before they went any further, Gabe stopped

on the path in front of her. His voice was quiet, and she had to strain to hear him. 'Later tonight when your work's done, I need to talk to you about something. I want to clear the air.' His words held a tone that she was unsure of. 'I want our . . . our friendship. . . to be built on honesty.'

'Oh, I get you.' Tam realised what he was worrying about. 'It's okay, Gabe. I already know that you booked to come over here and booked a hut before you met me. I've guessed why you didn't tell me. You didn't want to in case you decided after we went on our date, that you might change your mind and not want to see me again. It's okay. I think we had an excellent night out, didn't we?'

'We did. I missed you last night.'

Tam stood there hoping Gabe would take her in his arms. She didn't want to make the first move, but when he didn't move, she said quietly. 'I missed you too.'

'We'll talk later, okay. In the meantime, I think you might be needed down there. The music's stopped.'

Sure enough, the next thing Tam heard was

Rafe's voice on the microphone.

'Come on, Gabe. Whatever's bothering you, we'll sort it out later.' She grabbed his hand and pulled him along until they reached the crowded bar.

Chapter Twenty

Gabe

'Thanks, Mirabelle.'

Tam reached out and took a glass of wine from the tray that the woman was holding. 'Wine or beer, Gabe,' she asked. Her pretty eyes held his, and he tried to ignore the warmth that settled in his chest as she smiled up at him.

How could she look so beautiful and innocent when she had committed a major crime?

'I'm fine. You go and join your friends.' He tried not to respond and held himself stiff when she stood on her toes and brushed a kiss on his lips.

'I am so pleased you're here.' When she moved back her eyes were filled with hurt and confusion.

'I'll see you after the food is finished. Maybe we can go for a walk.'

'I'd like that.'

Tam pushed her way through the crowd and stood with the group of women at the end of the bar. The women linked arms as a voice with a cultured

English accent replaced the music.

'Ladies and gentlemen, may we have your attention please.'

Gradually the conversation faded away. Gabe turned. There were still boats approaching the island; it looked like the night was going to be a spectacular success. He was pleased for Tam and her friends. The island was smaller than he'd imagined, but it was beautiful. The house where he had found Tam cooking was not what he'd expected. It was a gracious old homestead nestled in the foothills of the mountain, the focal point of the island. There was nothing modern about the resort, the bar looked like it could have been lifted from a movie, and the huts he'd passed on the way up blended in with the rainforest behind.

'I'd like to welcome the head of Island Tourism, Natalie Worth, to say a few words before our Whitsunday mayor, Clifford Janisson, officially opens Ma Carmichael's resort.

A petite woman with dark hair took the microphone from the MC. 'Thank you, Rafe.' She looked around at the assembled crowd. 'Well, how fantastic is this?'

A cheer went up and glasses were raised by everyone in the bar.

'It's an honour to be here today and say a few words about this group of incredible women.' She turned and gestured to the group surrounding Tam. 'Many of you knew Violet Carmichael when she lived on Pentecost Island. She was born on the island and lived here for over eighty years. I have no doubt she would be extremely proud to see what her great-niece, Pippa, has achieved here over the past six months. Our region has been hit hard over the past few years, but developments like this will bring tourists back to our islands. Please raise your glasses to Pippa and her team to say a huge thank you for coming to the Whitsundays and giving life back to a beautiful island. I know as soon as I can get in, I'll be booking one of those fabulous huts. What a place to relax!' Natalie lifted her glass. 'To Ma Carmichael's, and the wonderful team who have created what we see tonight.' Another cheer went up as the guests toasted the team. 'Now, we're going to hear a few words from Pippa Carmichael, before Clifford officially opens the resort.'

Gabe watched as the tall woman left the group and took the microphone. Her hair was pale apricot, her skin was flawless, and her eyes were tipped up at the corners. She was stunning, but his attention strayed back to Tamsin. Her cheeks were glowing, and her smile was wide. As he stared, her gaze scanned the room and paused on him. Her beautiful smile was for him.

He smiled back at her, but his stomach churned as he worried about trying to get the truth out of her. And when he did, what was he going to do then? Gabe knew he only had one option; he would have to tell Lukas and she would be charged.

Shit. A case had never affected him like this before. He could usually stay uninvolved, but he had let Tamsin Jones under his skin.

Gabe had already booked a berth on the last trip back to Hamilton Island tonight, because he knew damn well the offer of a bed wouldn't hold once he'd talked to her.

His gaze switched to the woman on the microphone as she began to speak.

'Wow. Just wow. What else can I say?' Pippa's voice was strong and clear, but it was easy to see that she was overwhelmed. 'Thank you all so much for coming along tonight, and if every one of you comes out here to stay, we'll be booked out for years.' She reached up and swept back a loose strand of hair. 'I have some personal thank yous to make, plus a special announcement, but I promise I'll be quick. The fabulous food prepared by our world-class chef—Tamsin Jones—is hot and waiting to be brought down for your sampling pleasure.'

Pippa looked out over the crowd and it was clear that she was very emotional, and her shaking voice confirmed that as she continued. 'Almost twenty years ago I met two wonderful young girls. Those two girls have grown into strong and talented women and are my best friends in the whole world, Tamsin and Nell, come over here.'

Tamsin dabbed at her eyes as she walked over. The two women stood on either side of Pippa. 'This pair have stood by me through thick and thin and I am honoured to have them in my life. Early this year when I came up with the crazy idea of moving to a tropical island, they both supported me, left the world they knew, and moved to a ramshackle house on an almost deserted island. Not only are they friends, but they are also now financial partners in this venture.'

Gabe's stomach plummeted.

Bloody hell! Tamsin must have sold the ring to invest in the resort. He barely heard Pippa's words as she continued. His disappointment grew; Tamsin Jones wasn't the woman he'd thought. He couldn't have been more wrong about her.

'They have literally worked until they dropped, day and night, and we've now been joined by two other friends, who have done the same. Eliza and Evie, come over.' The two dark-haired women joined the group as Pippa continued. 'This week we have had some great news and I am delighted to announce that with these women, we have huge plans. We are expanding to build another fifteen huts in the next few months, plus a new restaurant building, and a day spa with our own Swiss beauty therapist. Come on over, Sienna.'

Sienna walked over and the six women put

their arms around each other's shoulders as they flanked Pippa.

'We *will* be successful, and I have no doubt that it is because of the strengths of our friendships, both new and old, that will let us make Ma Carmichael's the best resort in the islands.'

The cheer from the crowd was deafening.

'Only one more thank you.' Pippa stepped across to the man who was M.C. and Gabe assumed he was the Rafe that Tamsin spoke about. She took his hand in hers.

'I said before that we moved to an almost deserted island. I never knew that Aunty Vi had had a friend in her last months on her beloved island. Nor did I know that he would become my life partner. I'd like to thank my fiancé, Rafe, for being with me every step of the way. Thank you everyone, that's enough from me, and I'll hand over to Clifford, and then you can eat.'

The mayor gave a brief speech and announced the resort open, but Gabe was focused on Tamsin. No matter what she'd done he knew he couldn't get her out of his head.

Maybe the best thing to do was leave. Leave the island, book a flight, go back to Melbourne and put this whole week behind him. He was aware of Tamsin trying to get his attention as she walked out of the bar with the waitresses, but he looked away.

He had a decision to make.

Chapter Twenty-One

Tam put her hand to her chest and breathed a sigh of relief as the last of the empty plates went up to the kitchen. Everything had gone and the food had lasted the hour and a half, so there had been enough to feed the hordes.

The free drinks had stopped when the food came out. Another clever timing ploy of Pippa's to split the crowd between the bar and the food.

Nat and Rafe had been joined behind the bar by Eliza, Nell and Sienna, and the queue was six deep along the length of the wooden counter. Evie was clearing tables with Mirabelle and Tess. Amanda was carrying the platters up to the kitchen, and Cherry was washing up. A hand touched Tamsin's shoulder and she turned around with a smile. Her smile stayed there even though it wasn't Gabe.

'We've done good, Tam,' Pippa said. 'And *you* have excelled yourself. You wouldn't believe how many people have commented on the food. The manager of the Reef Hotel even asked if he could entice you away.'

'No way, not for anything he could offer. I'm here to stay.' She shot a quick grin at Pippa. 'Besides I have a wedding to cater for.'

'The first of many, I hope. I've had some enquiries already.'

'That's fantastic.'

'Yes, as soon as the restaurant is built, we'll move into the wedding business as well.'

'It's so exciting. Restaurant, weddings, day spa. We'll need a heap more staff. The four casuals have already told me that they'd love to work here.'

'We will. That's on the top of my list. Oh, and speaking of jobs, I met your Gabe before.'

'He's not my Gabe.' Tam bit her lip thinking of the cool reception she'd received from him. 'I think he's lost interest. But no matter. He's heading back to Melbourne, and I've got a business to help you run.'

'He said he's going to look for work up this way. I told him to catch up with Nat later. I think he's very interested. I thought how good you looked together when you walked in with him. And he hasn't taken his eyes off you all night.'

Tam shrugged. 'A nice guy, but a holiday fling.'

'As long as you're happy with however it pans out.'

'I am. I live on a tropical island; I have the best job in the world and my best friends are here too.'

'We made the right choice coming up here. Now go and get out of your work gear and leave the cleaning up to the casual staff. The guys are moving the tables out for dancing soon. Go and get glammed up and find Gabe. Just because it's a fling doesn't mean you can't enjoy yourself.' Tam laughed when Pippa winked at her. 'He was talking to Rafe last I saw him.'

##

Tam hurried back to the house, pulled her work clothes off, and slipped on her dress with the red, blue and green tropical print. She let her hair down, plumped up the curls, and tucked a red hibiscus behind her ear. With a spray of perfume, her jewellery on, and flat red sandals, she took a quick look in the mirror. Her eyes were bright, and her face was glowing, even without any of Sienna's magic.

What would tonight bring?

The thought of Gabe working up in the islands was one that excited her; as much as she had denied it to Pippa, she wasn't looking forward to him leaving. He had touched her heart; a heart that she had thought was immune to men.

On the way out she popped into the kitchen and was pleased to hear laughter as the two girls cleaned up. The kitchen was almost done, and everything was away, apart from a few trays on the table.

'Oh, well done, girls. Thanks so much.'

'We had fun,' Cherry said.

'And you've worked hard. Come on down to the bar when you're done, and I'll buy you a wine.'

'Thanks, we wondered if we could, seeing we were working. We're booked on the boat at eleven.' Amanda looked up from wiping the benches down.

'We're pretty laid-back around here,' Tam said. 'I'll see you in the bar in a while.' She shook her head as she walked back through the glade. There were people everywhere. A group sat at the table beneath the big mango tree and called out as she walked past. 'Great food, Tamsin. We'll be back soon.'

There were dozens of guests sitting on the beach that was lit by the tiki torches that Rafe and Nat had put every few metres. The bay was full of boats of all descriptions, and by the sound of the music coming across the water, some of the guests had already moved back onboard and were partying on.

There were still many partygoers at the bar as she stepped off the path. The music was loud, and she smiled as a Beach Boys' song came on, and those on the dance floor sang along.

Tam hummed under her breath as she looked around for Gabe, but there was no sign of him. On her second circuit around the dance floor, and then a look outside, disappointment kicked in.

She straightened her shoulders; nothing was going to spoil tonight. Turning to go back to the bar, she gasped as she bumped into a solid chest. Gabe grabbed her arms and held her steady.

'Whoa there.' His voice sent a familiar shiver

down her spine. Being this close to him brought back the memories of the other night in his bed.

'I was looking for you. Come and dance with me.' Tam grabbed Gabe's hand and forged a way through the crowd, just as a slow song came on. She smiled; good timing, this way she could be held close.

Pippa and Rafe were on the dance floor, and Pippa nodded as Gabe took Tam into his arms.

'Good playlist, Pip,' Tam said as Gabe held her. He reached for her right hand ready to waltz, and her ring caught on the front of his shirt.

Tam frowned as he stiffened; it was as though an electric shock went through him. He stood and stared at her hand as the music surrounded them. After a minute, he pulled her to him and began to move with the music. Gabe's heart thudded against her chest and she knew he was enjoying being close again as much as she was. Tam followed his lead, and eventually he put his head close to her. His breath whispered against her cheek.

'Who are you, Tamsin Jones? Are you the outgoing party girl I met this week, or are you the efficient chef who doesn't bat an eyelid at catering for a crowd of three hundred people? Or are you someone totally different? Someone I don't know?'

'You sound . . . disappointed, Gabe.'

He shook his head. 'Not disappointed, just curious.'

'About?'

'About you.' He lifted her hand and looked at the ring. 'I thought I had figured you out, but I was wrong. Very wrong.'

'What needs figuring out about me? I'm not very complicated.' Tam couldn't understand what was wrong. 'Did I go to your bed too soon?'

'No, of course not. That was a mutual decision. And an excellent one.' Finally, there was a bit of life in his voice. 'Can I ask you to do something for me?

'Depends what it is.'

'I have to go and make a phone call. Stay here, and don't dance with anyone else. I'll find you a chair and get you a drink, but there's something I have to do.'

Confusion filled Tam, but she decided to go with trust. Something that she wasn't very good at . . .

and hadn't been for a couple of years. 'Of course. I could do with that. I haven't sat down since we had lunch here about eight hours ago.'

'Have you had anything to eat? I'd hate to ply you with wine on an empty stomach.'

'Um, no.'

Gabe walked her off the dance floor and surprisingly found an empty table. 'Bubbles or wine?'

'I'm easy. Surprise me.'

Tam sat down at the table and five minutes later, she chuckled when Gabe returned with a bottle of wine, two glasses, and Nell behind him carrying a platter of hot food. But more importantly, he came back with a happy face.

'Nell saved you some food.'

Nell looked guilty. 'Don't be cross, but I put a few platters away for us all later.'

'I'm not cross. I'm starving.'

Nell put the platter down and sat beside Tam.

'Thank you,' Nell said as Gabe poured them each a glass of wine. 'Are you going to come to the party later, Gabe? Are you staying the night? I know Nat wants to have a chat to you. About some work.'

'Excellent. And yes, I hope so,' Gabe said. 'And Tamsin Jones. You stay right there. I'll be back soon.'

Tam stared after him as he hurried away.

'He's gorgeous, Tam,' Nell said. 'But you look . . . I don't know . . . maybe unsure. Isn't it working out?'

'I don't know, Nellie. Yes, I like him . . . more than I wanted to, but there's just something I can't put my finger on. Something not quite right.'

'Is it more because of your issue with what happened after Chad dumped you? A trust issue?'

Tam shrugged. 'Probably. But that's me. There's not a lot I can do about it.'

Nell leaned forward. 'There is you know. If you care about him, you could be honest.'

'What!' Tam almost shrieked. 'And tell him about Chad and what happened to me? No way. I haven't even told Pippa.'

Nell put her hand on Tamsin's. 'Take it from one who knows, Tam. I've been there and I know what a huge difference it's made to the load I was carrying when I told you about why I was so scared of strangers.'

'I'm not carrying a load.' Tam was cross. Suddenly, the happy mood and the anticipation of spending another night with Gabe had been replaced by that awful feeling she got when she thought about the time after Chad.

They sat there quietly drinking their wine. Tam pushed the tray of food away.

Her appetite was gone.

Chapter Twenty-Two

Gabe

Gobsmacked. That was the only word for how Gabe had felt when he'd seen the ring on Tamsin's hand.

Maybe followed by hope.

And maybe he'd jumped to too many hasty conclusions. His thoughts had been screwed since the minute he'd met her at the yacht club. He was going to ring Lukas and tell him he was off the case, and then he was going to tell Tamsin the truth about why he'd made sure he'd met her that night.

He walked over to the rocks at the side of the bay and pulled his phone out. The bay was quieter now, and there weren't as many small boats pulled up on the sand as there had been when he'd arrived.

Darkness surrounded him as he sat there, thinking about Tamsin and how she would take what he had to say. He put himself in the same position. If someone had been running checks on his background, and checking his bank balance, he'd be totally pissed.

And he knew she would be too. He'd try to

make her understand it was a job, but even he was becoming disillusioned with it more and more.

Gabe pulled out his phone and as soon as it came on, he saw there were three missed calls and one message from Lukas Werner. It had been so noisy in the bar he hadn't heard his phone buzz. He frowned and opened the message screen.

Pls call me asap. All good with ring. Close investigation.

What the hell?

He dialled Lukas and he picked up straight away.

'Gabe. Thanks for calling back so quickly. I wanted to let you know that you can pull the investigation. It's all been sorted.'

'Sorted? What do you mean by sorted?'

Lukas hesitated. 'I'm embarrassed about this, but I have to tell you. And please be assured that your account will be paid. Please know that what I am about to tell you is confidential.'

'Tell me.' His tone was short.

Lukas cleared his throat. 'The ring was never stolen. My mother gave it to Tamsin Jones as a gift.'

'A gift. A hundred-thousand-dollar gift?'

'Please understand. My mother became very close to Tamsin in a difficult situation. Tamsin supported my mother through a difficult time with an illness, and my mother reciprocated when Tamsin herself was in hospital.'

'She was ill?'

'Yes, my mother had breast cancer. Tamsin was by her side when my father couldn't be there. She used to take her to her chemotherapy sessions, and she was a wonderful support to her.'

'No, I meant was Tamsin ill?'

'Not ill, but she was in hospital and my mother stayed with her when she needed support.'

'What sort of support?

'Why are you so interested in this, Gabe? It has nothing to do with the case. Your involvement has finished now. Send me the final invoice and I'll make sure it is paid immediately. I'm sorry that we took up your time.'

'All right. I'll send it through tomorrow.'

'Oh, and one thing, I would like you to be aware of. I'm not happy about it, but my mother insisted that when she gave Tamsin the ring, she had no knowledge of the value of it. She said she wouldn't have accepted it had she known.

'I'm picking up that you may have formed a friendship with Tamsin. Perhaps in a roundabout way you could suggest she gets the ring valued. I'd hate to see it discarded for any reason.'

'That's correct, and if I get the opportunity, I will.'

'Thanks, Gabe and again, I'm sorry we wasted your time.'

'Lukas? Believe me when I say it wasn't wasted. Tamsin Jones is a wonderful woman. I would never have met her without this.'

'Gabe? If you're speaking to her again, please tell her my mother sends her love.'

##

Gabe stayed on the beach for a long time, trying to decide what he was going to say to Tamsin. Eventually he knew he had to leave. He'd be honest and follow his heart. The problem was how could he justify why he was investigating a stolen ring, when she thought it was worthless.

With a sigh, he left the beach and headed back to the bar. Tamsin was alone at the table where he'd left her. She smiled up at him as he stood beside her and reached her hand up to him.

'All done?' she asked.

He kept hold of her hand as he slid into the chair next to hers. Her fingers were warm, but the ring pressing against his hand was cold.

With a nod, he answered, 'I'm sorry I was so long. It was to do with my work, and I had to figure out how to deal with an issue.'

'We're both having a busy night. Have you had enough fresh air or are you happy to go for that walk now?'

'A walk would be good. When does the staff party start?'

'It will be a while yet. The last boat doesn't go back until eleven, so we'll have the bar open for at least another hour or so.'

Gabe let go of her hand and stood. 'Where will we go?'

'There's a good walk that goes up to the path that joins the track that goes to Red Wall, where people go rock climbing. Evie's put solar lights all the way up to the junction, but I haven't had a chance to go up there yet. There's a bit of a lookout there.'

'With this moon, it should be bright enough to see,' he said. 'Will you be right in those shoes?'

Tam nodded. 'Yes. Evie's levelled the path out apparently.'

'Let's go then.'

They walked in silence for the fifteen minutes that it took to walk up to the lookout. Gabe held Tamsin's hand the whole way, knowing that once he'd spoken to her there was a good chance she wouldn't want to have any more to do with him.

They stopped where the path split and the climb became steeper. Tamsin moved away from him and spread her arms gesturing to the view.

'Just look at that. Have you ever seen anything so beautiful?'

Gabe kept his eyes on her face. 'No, I have never seen anything so beautiful in my life.'

Her eyes were bright in the moonlight. 'I've only known you a very short time, but I can read you well. Something is wrong, isn't it.'

He turned away from her and stared over the water. There was a half moon, but it was still big enough to cast a golden glow on the inky water. 'Do you feel as though we have something special between us, Tamsin? Be honest. It is really important that we are honest.'

'Yes. I do. You have been in my head since I met you.' She reached out and splayed her fingers on his chest, and he reached up and closed his fingers over hers.

Gabe swallowed and closed his eyes. When he opened them and looked down, he could see the worry in her expression. Tamsin's eyes were shadowed, and her mouth was set in a straight line.

'You're going to tell me something I don't want to hear, aren't you?' Her voice rose a little. 'Are you married? Do you have a partner?'

'No. I was truthful with you. From a personal perspective.'

'Gabe, I don't know what you mean. What are you trying to tell me?'

'Tamsin, from the minute I stood beside you last Tuesday night, you have been in my heart. I want you to remember that when I tell you why I'm here. Why I came to your island, and why I sought you out.'

'Gabe?' Her voice was a whisper and she put her hand up to touch his face. 'You do care about me, don't you?'

The words were torn from him. 'More than you can know, and that's why I hesitate to be honest with you. I could just let it all go and you would never know, and I wouldn't see your hurt, but that wouldn't be fair to you. Or to me, I'd always know.'

'Know what?'

He placed his hand over hers that cupped his cheek. 'Can I kiss you before we talk?'

Tamsin stood on her toes, and her lips reached his before he could move. Gabe wrapped his arms around her, and her lips clung to his. He had never experienced such a sweet and giving kiss, and then she pulled away.

'Okay, now tell me.'

Gabe kept his voice steady. 'I'm a private investigator and I was given a job up here.'

'And what's that got to do with me?' she

asked.

'I breached my own rules. I got involved with the person I was investigating.'

She stepped back so quickly, he could feel the shock ricocheting through her body. 'Me? You were investigating me?' Tamsin's tone changed from shock to anger. 'You were investigating me, and you slept with me? You made me believe that you cared about me?'

'I do, and I did then. The only dishonest thing I have done was pretend I bought scallops in the bistro that night. That was a lie.'

Her laugh was bitter. 'So, what's the truth. Why were you investigating me?' Ironically, she lifted her hand and the ring flashed in the moonlight.

'I can't be specific because my client asked me not to divulge the information when the case was closed, but it was suspected that you had stolen something. It turned out tonight that the item was never stolen in the first place.'

Tamsin lifted her hand to her face and that damned ring flashed again. 'I have no idea what you're talking about, and I have no idea what I was suspected of stealing. All I know is that you pretended to be someone you're not.' Her head shook from side to side. 'Gabe, I could have dealt with anything but not that. You lied to me.'

She turned away, but he saw the tears welling in her eyes before she moved.

Her voice was muffled. 'I don't want to see you again. Ever. Go back to Melbourne and whatever it is you do. I can't forgive you, Gabe, no matter how much I care about you.'

Chapter Twenty-Three

Tamsin

By the time she ran down the hill and reached the resort, Tamsin had regained control of her emotions. If she kept the anger burning inside, she could hide how upset she was.

She had known there was something wrong as soon as Gabe had come down to the wharf to see them off the other day. At that point, she should have ended it. She should not have seen him again. Forgotten about him. That would teach her; she should have trusted her instincts.

Should, should, should.

When she approached the bar, she swallowed and wiped her eyes. She would not ruin Pippa's night. And she wouldn't let Gabe ruin it either.

Turning around, Tamsin walked back to the path with a determined step and waited for him to come down the hill. She could hear the stones rolling down the hill as she stood in the shadows waiting for him. When he reached the path that led to the jetty, he paused and looked over towards the bar. Despite her anger, her heart clenched.

He looked so sad. His mouth was set and as she watched he brought his hands up to his eyes.

'Gabe?' she said softly.

'Tamsin Jones?' he said in that deep voice she had come to love.

Yes, love. In less than a week, she knew this man so well, despite the lies he had told. She had seen past that, and if pushed she probably still could.

'If I tell you about me, and why I don't trust easily will you tell me the truth?' she asked.

Gabe walked over and stood close to her. 'I decided to follow you and tell you anyway. It might be breaching my employer's confidence, but I need to tell you. I want honesty between us.'

Tamsin shook her head. 'Two years ago, I put my trust in a man I thought I loved. And I thought he loved me. Chad told me I was fat, and I listened to him. He told me I was not as good a chef as he was, and I believed him. When I won an award, he told me it was only because the judges had agreed that it should go to a woman. I believed him.'

Gabe went to speak, but she held her hand up.

'Not long after the awards ceremony, I discovered I was pregnant. It wasn't planned but I was excited about having a child. I must have known deep down because I didn't tell him straight away and that was a wake-up call for me. If I really loved him, and he loved me, it would have been a joyous thing, even unplanned. I knew I didn't want Chad to be the father of my child, so I decided to go it alone. The same afternoon I discovered he was seeing another woman. I left my job, and I left the profession.'

Now it all made sense. 'And you went to work in a jewellery store. For the Werners.'

She frowned. 'How did you know that?'

'Lukas Werner hired me to find a missing ring.' Gabe reached down and took her hand. 'I found the ring, but I also found the woman of my dreams.'

Tamsin looked up at Gabe and saw nothing but truth in his eyes. 'Mrs Werner was like a mother to me. Within a week she guessed I was pregnant; she made sure I ate properly, and she'd leave the store every morning to buy me a milkshake. When I got the pains, I was alone, and I called her in the middle of the night.'

'What about Pippa and Nell?'

'I couldn't bring myself to tell them. And they were both having their own problems then. Mrs Werner sat with me all night in the hospital, and I miscarried.'

'She sounds like a wonderful woman. And I know that you did the same for her when she was ill. I also know now that she *gave* you that ring when they sold the business.'

'But I don't understand why you would be up here looking for it.'

'Let me tell you the rest of the story and Tamsin? Please believe what I say. I was going to drop the case. I knew you hadn't stolen anything. You are a good person, and that shines out of you. But I let circumstances cloud my judgement. You wore the ring to dinner, and then I heard that you had a share in the business. The one thing you will have a hard time forgiving is I accessed your bank accounts. I saw the money go in, and I saw the money go out. I assumed you had sold the ring to buy into the business. I'm sorry I misjudged you.'

Tam wrinkled her nose and looked down at

her hand. The offending ring winked blue in the moonlight. 'I still don't understand. Mrs Werner wouldn't forget she gave me the ring.'

'No, but she didn't tell her husband or son, so when they did an audit when they were finally putting the valuables into bank security it was flagged as being in stock, but there was no sign of it.'

'You said valuables though? Why would they hire a private investigator to search for a cubic zirconia, and why would you assume that it was worth one hundred thousand dollars?'

Tamsin held her hand up in the moonlight and looked at the ring. Slowly comprehension dawned and she widened her eyes as she looked up at Gabe. 'My God, is this real? Did Mrs Werner give me a valuable ring by mistake?'

'It was no mistake,' Gabe said quietly. 'She wanted you to have it. Lukas said she thought very highly of you. When the truth came out, he said that she knew it was valuable, and that she had taken it from her jewellery collection, not the store stock.'

Tam bit her lip. 'They were a lovely couple, but they were very disorganised in the store.' She reached out and put her hand on Gabe's chest. The ring twinkled in the soft light. 'If it wasn't for this ring, I would never have met you.'

Happiness began to rise in her chest as a slow smile lifted his lips. 'I can't judge you, Gabe, you were only doing your job. I might not agree with what you had to do, but like I said, it was your job.'

'Do you mean that? Even though I lied by omission, and I thought the worst of you? Can you forgive me?'

'There is nothing to forgive. Although you are going to have to kiss me a lot to make up for hacking my bank account.'

Gabe leaned down and his lips brushed hers. 'I can do that.'

Tamsin let out a gentle satisfied sigh. 'Is there anything else I should know?'

'I hacked your Facebook account too.'

'That would have been pretty boring.'

'It was,' he agreed as his mouth headed for hers again. 'Food photos.'

'Oh. and one more confession My surname isn't Brown.'

'What is it?'

Gabe's eyes gleamed with amusement as he held her gaze. 'Ah, would you believe it's Smith?'

Tam's laughter filled the small glade. 'Anything else I need to know before we go and join the party?'

'Only one more thing. You have to get that ring insured, sweetheart.'

The moonlight was blotted out as Gabe's lips claimed hers.

Epilogue

The second week after the huts opened, and there were four other guests on the island, Tamsin stayed in one of the huts with Gabe. She'd negotiated a three-day holiday with Pippa. The condition was that she would cook the dinners for the guests each evening, but the rest of the days and nights were hers.

Pippa and Nell had looked at her in disbelief the night of the bar opening, when she had asked for the time off, and then told them where she was going to stay.

'Do I get a staff discount?' Tam had asked with a giggle.

Pippa grinned at her. 'I'm sure we can work something out.' She'd jumped up from her chair and gone around the table and dropped a kiss on Gabe's cheek. 'Welcome to the Pentecost Island family. I hope you realise that you get the whole package that comes with Tam?'

'The whole package?' Gabe had asked.

'You get to put up with all of us. What do we say, girls?'

'All for one, and one for all,' they chanted together and burst into peals of laughter.

Rafe, Nat and Phillipe laughed with them. 'It's not as bad as they say, mate,' Nat said. 'Now I hear you're looking for a job, I might just have something for you.'

***

Gabe was lying beside Tamsin on one of the sun lounges on the beach in front of their hut. It was his last day on Pentecost Island before he flew to Melbourne to close up his unit and pack his gear. 'I'm going to sell my car too,' he said. 'There's no point having one if I'm working and living on Hamo.'

'True. There's no cars on the island,' she said. 'How long do you think you'll be gone?'

'I promise to be back within a week. It's going to be hard working on Hamo, and you being here.'

'We'll take it slowly,' Tam said. 'I'm going to be busy here with the plans for the restaurant and kitchen, and you and Nat are going to be busy setting up your new business.' Nat and Gabe had found a three-bedroom apartment on Hamilton Island and were going to rent it together.

'Do you think—'

Tamsin didn't hear what he thought as a shrill scream came from the other end of the beach.

'No, no, no,' Evie yelled at the man standing in front of her. 'I won't.'

Gabe was on his feet in an instant and running across the sand with Tamsin close behind him.

'Who is he?' she asked as they ran towards Evie.

'It's the guy staying in the hut beside us, he arrived on the morning boat,' Gabe replied.

By the time they got to her, Evie was crouched on the ground, rocking on her heels as sobs shuddered through her.

The guy was standing over her, his hands spread almost in supplication. 'Please, Evie, you have to.'

Gabe grabbed his arm and pulled him away as Tamsin crouched on the ground beside her friend.

Shock ran through her. Evie's lips were bloodless, and the colour had leached from her face. Tears rolled down her face, and her voice was almost childlike as she grabbed onto Tamsin's hand.

'Tam make him go away. Please, please make him go away. I can't take it.'

THE END

Why is the usually calm and serene Evie upset? Come back and visit Pentecost Island as the friends band together to support her. Can Pippa, Eliza, Nell, Tamsin, and Sienna help Evie make a decision that could change her life, and save the life of another?

All for one, and one for all.

Evie sailed into life at Pentecost Island excited to have a place to belong after ten years of living alone on her boat. She uses her skills to landscape Ma Carmichael's Resort and cements her friendship with the girls on the island.

When Jed Stephenson, her brother's best friend— who also happens to be Evie's ex-husband— turns up on Pentecost Island to convince Evie it is time to go back home to her family, she is faced with a choice that may mean the difference between life and death for someone she once loved.

Can Jed break through the defences of the woman he has never stopped loving?

Come and spend some more time with the girls on Pentecost Island.

OTHER BOOKS from ANNIE

Whitsunday Dawn
Undara
Osprey Reef
East of Alice
Porter Sisters Series
Kakadu Sunset
Daintree
Diamond Sky
Hidden Valley
Larapinta
Kakadu Dawn
Pentecost Island Series
Pippa
Eliza
Nell
Tamsin
Evie
Cherry
Odessa
Sienna
Tess
Isla

The Augathella Girls Series
Outback Roads
Outback Sky
Outback Escape
Outback Wind
Outback Dawn
Outback Moonlight
Outback Dust
Outback Hope

Sunshine Coast Series
Waiting for Ana
The Trouble with Jack
Healing His Heart
Sunshine Coast Boxed Set

The Richards Brothers Series
The Trouble with Paradise
Marry in Haste
Outback Sunrise
Richards Brothers Boxed Set
Bondi Beach Love Series
Beach House
Beach Music
Beach Walk
Beach Dreams
The House on the Hill

Second Chance Bay Series
Her Outback Playboy
Her Outback Protector
Her Outback Haven
Her Outback Paradise
The McDougalls of Second Chance Bay Boxed Set
Love Across Time Series
Come Back to Me
Follow Me
Finding Home
The Threads that Bind
Love Across Time 1-4 Boxed Set
Bindarra Creek
Worth the Wait
Full Circle
Secrets of River Cottage
Four Seasons Short and Sweet
Ten Days in Paradise
Follow the Sun
Others
Deadly Secrets
Adventures in Time
Silver Valley Witch
The Emerald Necklace
Christmas with the Boss
Her Christmas Star
An Aussie Christmas Duo (two Christmas novellas)
A Clever Christmas

Acknowledgements

A special thank you to my wonderful editor and critique partner, Susanne Bellamy, and my eagle-eyed proof-readers, Roby Aiken, Nicki Edwards, Anna Welch and Kristen Woolgar.

About the Author

Author of the Year Ausrom Readers' Choice 2014

Best Established Author Ausrom Readers' Choice 2015

Finalist for Author of the Year, Book of the Year, Cover of the Year, Ausrom Readers' Choice 2016

Best Established Author, Ausrom Readers' Choice 2017

Book of the Year (Whitsunday Dawn) Ausrom Readers' Choice Awards 2018

Annie lives in Australia, on the beautiful north coast of New South Wales. She sits in her writing chair and looks out over the tranquil Pacific Ocean. She has fulfilled her lifelong dream of becoming an author and is producing books at a prolific rate.

She writes contemporary romance and loves telling the stories that always have a happily ever after. She lives with her very own hero of many years and they share their home with Toby, the naughtiest dog in the universe, and Barney, the rag doll kitten, who hides when the grandchildren come to visit.
Stay up to date with her latest releases at her website:
http://www.annieseaton.net

If you would like to stay up to date with Annie's releases, subscribe to her newsletter on her website.